in the
woods

BOOKS BY THIS AUTHOR

Comes a Horseman
Germ
Deadfall
Deadlock

DREAMHOUSE KINGS SERIES

1 House of Dark Shadows
2 Watcher in the Woods
3 Gatekeepers
4 Timescape
5 Whirlwind – Available January 2010

watcher in the woods

BOOK TWO OF DREAMHOUSE KINGS

ROBERT LIPARULO

THOMAS NELSON

Since 1798

NASHVILLE   DALLAS   MEXICO CITY   RIO DE JANEIRO

Published in Nashville, Tennessee, by Thomas Nelson. Thomas Nelson is a registered trademark of Thomas Nelson, Inc.

Thomas Nelson, Inc. books may be purchased in bulk for educational, business, fund-raising, or sales promotional use. For information, please e-mail SpecialMarkets@ThomasNelson.com.

Publisher's Note: This novel is a work of fiction. Names, characters, places, and incidents are either products of the author's imagination or used fictitiously. All characters are fictional, and any similarity to people living or dead is purely coincidental.

Page design by Mandi Cofer
Map design by Doug Cordes

ISBN 978-1-59554-728-6 (trade paper)
ISBN 978-1-59554-742-2 (trade paper SE)

Library of Congress Cataloging-in-Publication Data

Liparulo, Robert.
        Watcher in the woods / Robert Liparulo.
            p. cm. — (Dreamhouse Kings ; bk. 2)
        Summary: Twelve-year-old David and his family search for their
    kidnapped mother in the many different time period portals of their
    home, but when a stranger appears and tries to force them to sell the
    house, their desperation reaches new heights.
        ISBN 978-1-59554-496-4 (hardcover)
        [1. Time travel—Fiction. 2. Dwellings—Fiction. 3. Family life—California—Fiction.
    4. California—Fiction. 5. Horror stories.]
    I. Title.
    PZ7.L6636Wat 2008
    [Fic]—dc22

                                                                                2008009200

Printed in the United States of America
13 14 QG 9 8

THIS ONE'S FOR ISABELLA

"Ain't nothing sweeter"

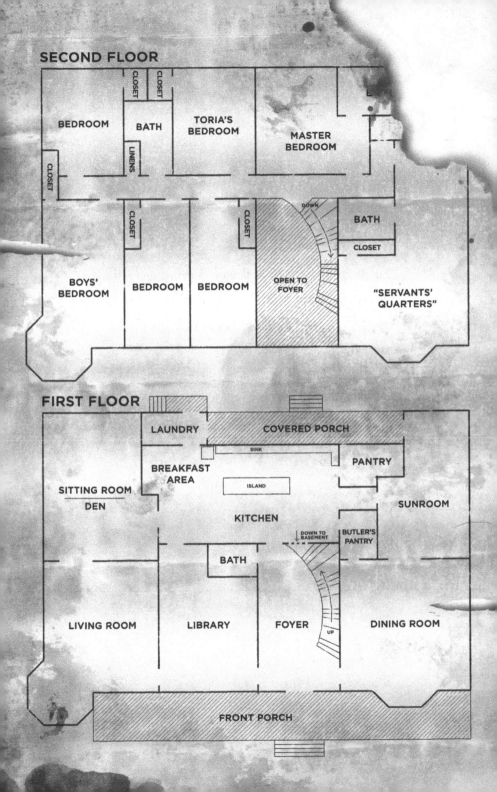

"You watched these people go through their lives and just had a feeling that they existed outside the usual laws of nature."

—CHARLES SPALDING

"I'm watching you, always watching."

—ROZ, *Monsters Inc.*

CHAPTER

one

At twelve years old, David King was too young to die. At least *he* thought so.

But try telling that to the people shooting at him.

He had no idea where he was. When he had stepped through the portal, smoke immediately blinded him. An explosion had thrown rocks and who-knew-what into his face. It shook the floor and knocked him off his feet. Now he was on his hands and knees on a hardwood floor. Glass and splinters dug into his palms. Somewhere, all kinds of guns were firing. Bullets zinged overhead, thunking into walls—bits of flying plaster stung his cheeks.

Okay, so he wasn't sure the bullets were meant for him. The guns seemed both near and far. But in the end, if he were hit, did it matter whether the shooters meant to get him or he'd had the dumb luck to stumble into the middle of a firefight? He'd be just as dead.

The smoke cleared a bit. Sunlight poured in from a school-bus-sized hole in the ceiling. Not just the ceiling—David could see attic rafters and the jagged and burning edges of the roof. Way above was a blue sky, soft white clouds.

He was in a bedroom. A dresser lay on the floor. In front of him was a bed. He gripped the mattress and pushed himself up.

A wall exploded into a shower of plaster, rocks, and dust. He flew back. Air burst from his lungs, and he crumpled again to the floor. He gulped for breath, but nothing came. The stench of fire—burning wood and rock, something dank and putrid—swirled into his nostrils on the thick, gray smoke. The taste of cement coated his tongue. Finally, oxygen reached his lungs, and he pulled it in with loud gasps, like a swimmer saved from drowning. He coughed out the smoke and dust. He stood, finding his balance, clearing his head, wavering until he reached out to steady himself.

A hole in the floor appeared to be trying to eat the bed. It was listing like a sinking ship, the far corner up in the air, the corner nearest David canted down into the hole. Flames had found the blankets and were spreading fast.

Outside, machine-gun fire erupted.

David jumped.

He stumbled toward an outside wall. It had crumbled, forming a rough, V-shaped hole from where the ceiling used to be nearly to the floor. Stumps of bent rebar jutted out of the plaster every few feet.

More gunfire, another explosion. The floor shook.

Beyond the walls of the bedroom, the rumble of an engine and a rhythmic, metallic *click-click-click-click-click* tightened his stomach. He recognized the sound from a dozen war movies: a tank. It was rolling closer, getting louder.

He reached the wall and dropped to his knees. He peered out onto the dirt and cobblestone streets of a small village. Every house and building was at least partially destroyed, ravaged by bombs and bullets. The streets were littered with chunks of wall, roof tiles, even furniture that had spilled out through the ruptured buildings.

David's eyes fell on an object in the street. His panting breath froze in his throat. He slapped his palm over his mouth, either to stifle a scream or to keep himself from throwing up. It was a body, mutilated almost beyond recognition. It lay on its back, screaming up to heaven. Male or female, adult or child, David didn't know, and it didn't matter. That it was human and *damaged* was enough to crush his heart. His eyes shot away from the sight, only to spot another body. This one was not as broken, but was no less horrible. It was a young woman. She was lying on her stomach, head turned with an expression of surprised disbelief and pointing her lifeless eyes directly at David.

He spun around and sat on the floor. He pushed his knuckles into each eye socket, squeegeeing out the wetness. He swallowed, willing his nausea to pass.

His older brother, Xander, said that he *had* puked when he first saw a dead body. That had been only two days ago—in the Colosseum. David didn't know where the portal he had stepped through had taken him. Certainly *not* to a gladiator fight in Rome.

He squinted toward the other side of the room, toward the shadowy corner where he had stepped into . . . wherever this was . . . *whenever* it was. Nothing there now. No portal. No passage home. Just a wall.

He heard rifle shots and a scream.

Click-click-click-click-click . . . the tank was still approaching.

What had he done? He thought he could be a hero, and now he was about to get shot or blown up or . . . something that amounted to the same thing: dead.

Dad had been right. They weren't ready. They should have made a plan.

Click-click-click-click-click.

David rose into a crouch and turned toward the crumbled wall.

I'm here now, he thought. *I gotta know what I'm dealing with, right? Okay then. I can do this.*

He popped up from his hiding place to look out onto the street. Down the road to his right, the tank was coming into town over a bridge. Bullets sparked against its steel skin. Soldiers huddled behind it, keeping close as it moved forward. In turn, they would scurry out to the side, fire a rifle or machine gun, and step back quickly. Their targets were to David's left, which meant he was smack between them.

Figures.

At that moment, he'd have given anything to redo the past hour. He closed his eyes. Had it really only been an hour? An hour to go from his front porch to here?

But in the house where he lived, stranger things had happened . . .

CHAPTER

63 MINUTES AGO
SUNDAY, 6:48 A.M.
PINEDALE, CALIFORNIA

Following Toria, his nine-year-old sister, David stepped through the front door onto the porch. Xander sat there on the steps next to Dad, watching the sun wash the nighttime out of the sky. Toria went down a step and sat on their father's other side, leaning her head into him.

Dad put his arm around her and squeezed her close.

David looked at his brother.

Xander had stormed out of the house, furious at Dad for not telling them he had known all along that the house they had moved into four days earlier was dangerous. He didn't look quite as angry now, and David's heart lifted when Xander smiled.

"We're going to rescue Mom," Xander said.

Mom. David's concern for her was like a knife in his chest. Less than two hours ago she had been taken—kidnapped into one of the other worlds that lay hidden within their new house. He had watched a man carry her away. He and Xander had tried to stop him, but the intruder was too big, too powerful.

Then Dad had confessed that his own mother had been taken into a portal the very same way, when Dad was only seven years old. They had never found her. His father, Grandpa Hank, had feared for his children and his own sanity and taken the family away. Xander had gone through the roof. He'd screamed that he wouldn't leave until they'd found Mom, but David was afraid Dad wouldn't let them stay, knowing it wasn't safe. Now, it seemed Xander and Dad had agreed: they would stay.

David scanned the front of the house.

She's not yours, he thought. *We're coming for her, you hear?*

His eyes dropped to his sister's face, then over to his dad's. They felt it too, he could tell. They were up to this challenge. He looked at Xander's eyes and saw hope there, and determination.

David nodded. "Let's do it."

Xander reached for the railing and pulled himself up. "Good idea, Dae," he said, and bolted up the stairs.

David was right on his heels.

"Whoa, whoa, guys," Dad called out. "Xander!"

Xander kept moving. He pushed through the front door and took the stairs three at a time. David rushed to keep up.

Behind them, Dad yelled, "Xander! David! Stop!"

Xander turned on the landing, fire in his eyes. "*What?*"

David stopped two steps from the top.

"Where are you going? What are you doing?"

"Rescuing Mom," Xander said in the same tone he would use to explain that water was wet.

"We're going to do that, son, absolutely. But we need a plan."

"I *have* a plan!" Xander yelled.

It scared David how forcefully Xander said it.

"I'm going over," Xander continued. "And I'm going to keep going over until I find her."

Going over.

Since moving into the house, their lives just kept getting weirder and weirder. It had begun with the discovery that the second-floor linen closet was more than a storage place for towels and bedsheets: it was a portal to a locker at the Pinedale Middle and High School. Then he and Xander had followed an intruder in their home through a secret door in the wall.

There they'd found a flight of stairs to a third floor—a twisting hallway with doors on either side. Beyond each door was a . . . well, that was another thing. The new world they lived in came with its own vocabulary: an *antechamber* was what lay beyond each of the twenty doors in the upstairs hallway. It was a small room containing a bench and a selection of items—clothing, tools, weapons.

Set in the opposite wall of each antechamber was another door, always locked. Unlocking it required putting on or picking up some of the items. Beyond that door was a *portal*, a passage-way from their house to one of the other worlds and back.

World was the word they used to describe the different times and places they could step into from their house. Xander had done it first. He had put on a helmet and chain mail, picked up a sword, and stepped into the Colosseum—right in the middle of a gladiator fight. Their father had barely managed to rescue him.

And *going over* or *crossing over* was the term he and Xander had begun using to describe stepping through a portal to a different world.

"It's not that simple," Dad said.

"It *is* that simple," Xander shot back. He ran down the hall toward the secret door.

"Xander!" As Dad flew past David, he said, "Stay here." He disappeared around the corner.

David threw a quick glance at Toria, who was standing in the entryway. He knew her expression mirrored his own:

open mouth, wide eyes. He thought of saying something, then he turned and bolted after his father and brother. He reached the hidden stairway to the third floor and clambered up. Toria was right behind him.

The first antechamber door was open. David could hear Xander's and Dad's voices:

"Let me go!"

"Just wait! Wait, I said!"

David slammed into the door frame. Xander was on his back on the floor; Dad was sitting on him, gripping Xander's shirt in his fists.

Tears streamed out of Xander's eyes. "You don't care!" he yelled. "You *let* her get taken!"

Dad pulled Xander up so they were nose to nose. Dad opened his mouth, then snapped it closed, pressing his lips tight. He stared into Xander's eyes, and slowly his face softened. He whispered, "Don't you think I want to do exactly what you're trying to do? Don't you think I want to go in after her too, just snatch her back? I do, Xander, I do. It's just . . ." He looked up at David and Toria, standing in the doorway. "It's not that easy. I've done this before. If we have any chance to find your mother—"

"*If?*" Toria said.

Dad looked at her sadly. "If we have any chance, any chance at all, it lies in being smart about it." He lowered his hands until Xander's head was back on the floor. "We can't just go crashing over. It's too dangerous. Your mother wouldn't want that." Dad stood and extended a hand to Xander.

Xander glared at it, pushed himself up, and stood. He wiped the tears off his face, then he sat on the bench and looked at the floor.

When neither of them spoke, David said, "So . . . what do we do?"

"Now," Xander said. "Not later—*now*."

Dad took a deep breath and looked around the room. "What did you see when the guy took Mom? In the room, I mean?"

"It was *snowy*," David said. "There was a white parka . . . and snowshoes . . . gloves . . ."

"Goggles," Xander added.

"Okay, so maybe the Arctic," Dad said, thinking.

"But she didn't stay there," Xander said.

Their father cocked his head. "What do you mean?"

"She didn't stay there long," Xander said, sounding frustrated.

David said, "We heard her in the hall. We ran out and she was trying to come through another door. Something . . ." A lump in his throat choked his words. "Something pulled her back in."

Dad stepped over to him and combed his fingers through David's hair. "A different room? Not the Arctic one?"

"We went in the antechamber," David said. "There were pirate things. A sword and a three-cornered hat."

"Like Johnny Depp's in *Pirates of the Caribbean*," Xander said. Leave it to him to put it in movie terms

Their father's puzzled look deepened.

"What's it mean?" Xander asked.

Dad shook his head. "Grandpa Hank said he thought there was a way to go from world to world without coming back through the house each time."

"Other portals?" David asked.

"I don't know. If so, he never found them. But if it's true, she could be anywhere, in any world."

"We already figured that out," Xander said.

"And if there are other portals," Dad said slowly, thinking it through, "it'd be like a combination lock. Every new portal would make the number of possible worlds she could have gone to increase exponentially."

Xander looked at him hard. "What are you saying? That it's impossible?" He stood. "We haven't even started, and you're *giving up?*"

"No, no," Dad said. He reached out and laid his hand on Xander's shoulder. Xander pulled away, but Dad continued: "It's just that we have even more work ahead of us than I thought."

"So what do we do?" David said again.

"Let's look for those worlds," Dad said. "The Arctic one and the pirates. She's probably not in either one, not anymore, but it's a place to start."

Xander said, "It'll be faster if we split up. David and me. You and Toria."

Dad studied him. "Xander, look at me," he said. "Can I trust you?"

David watched Xander meet Dad's gaze.

"More than I can trust *you*," his brother said.

CHAPTER

"Why are you being so mean to Dad?" David asked.

Xander didn't look away from the items hanging from hooks in the antechamber they stood in. Dad and Toria had left to find notepads and pens to catalog the rooms. "What do you mean?"

David mimicked his brother: "'More than I can trust *you.*'"

"It's true," Xander said.

"Dad made a mistake, that's all."

"His mistake got Mom kidnapped. Don't you understand? We may never see her again."

"We will," David said quietly. His heart felt like a cannonball in his chest. He surveyed the things in the room. "Doesn't look like any big deal," he said.

There was a leather jacket, a beret, a sheathed knife, a belt of rifle cartridges. On the bench lay a rolled-up paper and a crumpled pack of cigarettes.

"Hard to tell," Xander said. He elbowed David's arm. "You should know that, going over the way you did."

Xander was right. You couldn't judge a world's safeness by the items in the antechamber. After Xander's trip to the Colosseum, David had wanted to try it. They had chosen a room with clothes and tools that had seemed even more harmless than the ones here. And David had stepped smack into the middle of three hungry tigers and a tribe of fierce hunters.

He lifted the leather jacket off its hook. It was heavy, old, and wrinkled. He slipped it on.

Xander smiled and said, "'No man left behind.' That's from *Black Hawk Down*."

"No woman left behind," David amended. He snatched the beret off the hook in front of him. It was big on his head, but he left it propped there, tilted down over one eyebrow. He said, "Xander, you know Dad feels the same way. He won't leave without Mom."

Xander didn't respond.

David said, "He loves Mom."

"He should have thought of that before bringing us here."

"He didn't think it would happen so fast. He thought he could protect us."

"He was wrong."

"He said when he lived here as a kid, the weird stuff didn't start happening for months. He thought he had time to make it safe, to figure it out."

The muscles in his brother's face seemed to tighten. David didn't like to see him looking so stern, so angry.

"He loves Mom," David repeated, whispering.

Xander sat on the bench. "Look," he said. "I know he does, and I know he didn't mean for any of this to happen. But it did—because of him. He loves us, too, and that's why he might try to get us out of here, thinking it's best. But it won't be, not without Mom."

David picked up the pack of cigarettes. He said, "This is *open*. And there are cigarettes missing. Weird."

"Why is that weird?"

David turned the pack over in his hands. The cigarettes inside felt like bones underneath a thin layer of skin. "It makes me wonder whose they were. What does he think happened to his pack of smokes?"

Xander shrugged, clearly not interested.

"And look," David said, holding the package up. "What language is that?"

"*Flor belmonte . . . extra-vergé,*" Xander read. He shrugged again. "Italian?"

David examined the pack, then slipped it into the jacket pocket. He looked at the door leading to the world where the jacket, beret, and cigarettes belonged. Had he picked up enough of them to unlock the door? Hadn't they determined that it took only three items from the antechamber to open the portal door? He looked sideways at Xander, who was reaching for the roll of paper.

Giving in to curiosity, knowing he shouldn't, David gripped the door handle and turned it. The door flew open as though pushed from the other side. A whoosh of warm air swept in.

"Hey!" Xander said. David sensed him stepping up behind him. He felt a tug as Xander's hand grabbed the collar of the leather jacket. "*David!*"

"I'm just looking," David said. But really there was nothing to see. Sometimes what lay beyond the doorway was fairly clear, as when they were able to see the jungle floor before David stepped through. But before Xander found himself in the Colosseum, they had seen the world on the other side as indistinct shapes. It was like that now, like peering through a steamed-up shower door.

A blurry object flashed past, causing David to jump. "Whoa!"

Another figure passed by on the other side of the threshold. This one was more distinct—dark hair framing a white face, dark clothes.

"People," Xander said.

"Doing what?"

More and more figures went past, moving right to left. A child went by, everything about him clear as tap water. David saw fear in the boy's eyes as he turned to look back over his shoulder. And yet, the person whose hand he was holding was blurry and indistinct.

"It's like we're seeing it through a camera lens," Xander said. "And somebody is playing with the focus."

The sound coming through was no better. Most of it was a garbled murmur. Now and then words came through. The syllables were sharp, but David didn't understand the language. A low *boom* sounded like the beating of a drum.

"A parade?" David wondered out loud.

"Shut the door," Xander said. "Wait for Dad."

More faces—in and out of focus.

"Hold on," David said. "I want to see more. Maybe I can figure out what they're doing."

"Don't move," Xander said, releasing David's collar.

David glanced back to watch Xander step into the hallway. "Dad!" his brother called.

Dust and smoke drifted into the little room. It smelled like fireworks on the Fourth of July. The angle of the view through the doorway seemed to be getting higher. David could see more people, mostly their heads now, not their bodies. He remembered Xander telling him that he had watched the jungle moving past the doorway before he jumped in to rescue David from the tigers. Whatever these portals were, they were not locked in one place. They moved, as though with a breeze or caught in an ocean current.

A face came into focus and immediately blurred. David's heart jumped into his throat. The glimpse had been enough.

"Mom," he whispered. Then he shouted it: "Mom! Xander! I saw Mom!" He leaned his shoulder into the door frame, hoping for another glimpse.

Xander raced up to him. "Where? David, where?"

"She went past! Xander, it was her!"

"Are you sure?"

"I'm sure! I'm sure!"

Xander went back into the hallway and yelled, "Dad! Dad!" His voice was shrill, panicky. His eyes were wide. He was shifting his gaze down the hall, back to David, down the hall again. David realized Xander was as clueless about what to do as he was.

He watched the throng of people in the other world start to thin out. The perspective of the doorway rose higher and farther away. He could no longer see the spot where he thought his mother was.

"Xander, I . . . she . . ." He turned his head.

Xander was looking at him, reading him perfectly. "No!"

"Wait for me!" David said and stepped through the portal.

CHAPTER

four

And so he found himself staring over the crumbling wall at
an approaching tank.

Click-click-click-click-click.

Its turret rotated toward him. When the big barrel was
pointed directly at him—all he could see of it was a black
hole—it stopped. Fire and smoke erupted from it.

David dropped to the floor, knowing the wall would be like
wet paper to the incoming shell. He squeezed his eyes shut.

Here lies a boy named David King, he thought, the image of his headstone filling his mind. *Food for worms because he did a stupid thing.*

He heard the whine of the shell as it cut through the air over his head. The explosion was farther away than he expected. The floor shook and dropped down a foot. Plaster and rock rained over him.

He cracked open an eye. The shell had gone through the bedroom's crumbled exterior and interior walls, sailing right through into the attic beyond. Two feet lower and he'd be as gone as the section of roof above his head, through which he could see the blue sky beyond.

The hum of the tank's turret started again. It was turning its cannon away from him! He brushed the debris off his face and shoulders, then took off the beret and slapped at his hair, kicking up thick plumes of white powder. He draped the beret back over his head and lifted his eyes over the top of a shattered wall. Men were crouched behind rubble and smoldering vehicles, shooting at the tank and the soldiers following it. Beyond this scattering of ragtag combatants, a bullet-pocked door cracked open and a woman peered out. She was not his mother, but he could see people crowded in the room behind her. This must be where the fleeing villagers had wound up. Maybe his mother was among them.

The tank boomed out a shell. David watched it flash into one of the cars the resistance fighters were hiding behind. It exploded. He saw bodies fly but quickly told himself that they were just parts of the car. The explosion rattled the façade of the building nearest it: a section of it, from ground to roof and ten feet wide, crumbled and fell, exposing the joists of the second floor and attic rafters. He caught a glimpse of an upper-floor bedroom similar to the one he was in, before smoke and dust obscured it.

Keeping low, he pushed away from the wall, then ran out of the bedroom and down a narrow flight of wooden stairs. They emptied into what used to be a pub. Most of the front wall was gone, pounded to dust. So were half the bar, tables, and chairs. A corner of the upstairs bed, the one that was burning, poked through the ceiling. Swatches of fiery bedding fell through. The heavier pieces plunged down like meteorites; lighter ones floated gently down like leaves from a flaming tree. Already the wood floor had ignited in a dozen spots. Smoke churned against the ceiling, filled the space with gray fog.

David coughed and coughed again. His throat was raw from the heat and smoke. His eyes stung. His lungs demanded fresh air. He dropped to his hands and knees and scampered across the floor, giving the flames a wide berth. He jumped over the rubble at the front of the building. Twisted rebar caught his foot, and he crashed down. He fell on top of jagged chunks of concrete and flipped over, landing in the street. By the time he caught his breath and blinked away the smoke and tears, three rifles were trained on him.

He threw up his hands. "Don't shoot me, please."

The faces behind the rifles twisted in confusion.

"*Qui êtes-vous? Identifiez-vous!*" one of the men shouted.

Oh, crap. David shook his head.

One man turned to the others, "*C'est seulement un enfant.*"

Enfant! David recognized the word from French class. It meant *child.*

"Yes, yes!" he said, nodding his head vigorously. "*Oui . . . enfant, enfant.*"

The tank belched out another round. The three men hunched down. David bowed his head, covering it with his arms. The explosion was a good fifty yards away. Still, debris zinged past David like buckshot. Something hit him in the calf. He grabbed it in pain, sure that he would find his flesh ripped open. It felt intact, so he opened one eye and looked. His jeans were not torn. No blood.

The fighters had forgotten him. Two of them were firing their rifles from around the back of a wrecked truck. The other had stepped onto the twisted bumper to get the barrel of a machine gun high enough to shoot over their own barricade.

David scrambled up. He limped down the block and across the street toward the door he had seen the woman open. Gunfire popped behind him. Divots of plaster ripped from the building on his right. Bullets sparked off the cobblestone on his left. He slammed into the red painted door. The thumb lever of the handle would not depress. He pounded on the door. Thinking of nothing else to say, he cried, *"Enfant, enfant!"*

The door opened an inch. An eye inspected him. Then it swung wide, and he was pulled inside. The air was stuffy and hot. There was an awful odor, which David knew must be sweat, but the first thing that came to his mind was *fear*. The room was crowded with women, children, and old men. Several people asked him questions he didn't understand. He shook his head and nodded, all the while moving to take in every face.

Then he saw the back of her head, the familiar color of her hair—golden yellow, like turning leaves. But this woman wore a dress. His mother had been taken in her nightgown. Of course, she would have found other clothes by now. He stepped around an old man whose shaking hands wanted to touch him, around two children not much younger than himself. Their cheeks were wet with tears. One of them was glassy-eyed, his face slack with shock. The other spoke to David urgently, repeating a line over and over. David frowned at him and shook his head.

His mother was huddled in a group of women.

"Mom!" David yelled. He supposed the word was similar to the one these other children would use. Many heads turned his way, all offering blank or hopeful stares.

His mother noticed the gazes the other women were giving him. She turned. As she did, she spoke rapidly to someone he could not see. His heart sank. She was speaking in French.

Her resemblance to his mother was undeniable, and his heart

skipped for a moment as he let himself think that he had been right. But he wasn't.

The woman responded to the disappointment on his face with sadness of her own. Softly she said, *"Avec qui êtes-vous, fils? Est-ce que je peux vous aider?"*

The ache in David's chest made him feel that his heart had turned into a plastic lump. It radiated out, transforming him into a plastic boy. He could not speak, he could not move; he didn't know if he was breathing or blinking. He had been so sure. . . . Deep in his mind he had already embraced her, told her how much he missed her, had taken her hand and brought her home.

A tear rolled down his cheek, and he knew his bottom lip was quivering.

The woman's frown deepened. *"Vous êtes si triste."* She held out her arms and stepped toward him.

He backed away, turned, and ran for the door. He was only half-aware of pushing people out of his way. He collided with the boy who had spoken to him. The boy yelled and went down. At the door, an old woman blocked his way. She shook a gnarled finger at him, scolding him with words he didn't understand. He shook his head back and forth, back and forth, trying to rid his mind of his lost hope, his sorrow, and even his being there.

One word formed out of it all and bounced around inside his skull like a racquetball: *Stupid . . . stupid . . . stupid . . .*

He shoved his shoulder between the old woman and the door. He flipped a dead bolt, pulled the door open, and went through.

Gunfire, screams, oily smoke. Behind him, voices rose in alarm. Several women called out to him: "*Enfant!*" and "*Garçon!*"

He stumbled into the street. Blinking hard to clear his vision, he looked back. The old woman scowled at him, cold to his feelings, calloused by the disrespect of youth. Faces behind her expressed worry and concern. More of them joined in a chorus, calling him back to safety. The old woman held on to the door. She gave him one last scowl and slammed it shut.

CHAPTER

five

The tank had come off the bridge. Now it was rumbling toward David on the town's main street. Under massive splatterings of mud and grime, it was painted in a camouflage pattern. On the front, where an emblem would have been on a car, was painted a white and black cross—David recognized the symbol of the German army.

I'm in World War II, he thought. *More than half a century before I was born.*

While the tank headed directly toward him, the gunners inside and the soldiers behind were occupied by something off to the side. Machine guns and rifles spat bullets in that direction. The tank's turret and cannon barrel slowly rotated toward the conflict. Bullets pinged against the side of the tank, kicking up tiny sparks.

Over the shooting and the rumble of the tank—sounds much louder than movies made them out to be—a voice reached his ears: "*Vous, là, sortez de la manière! Déplacez-la, garçon!*"

He turned away from the tank to see a man waving at him from farther up the street. The man wore a beret like his own and held a rifle. Beside him, behind a wall of rubble, more faces peered. The man waved his free hand high in the air as if swatting at flies. "*Sortez de la manière!*"

David was standing between the oncoming German army and the French Resistance. A breeze passed him. He felt it in his arms and hair, but it had not touched his face, and he realized it was not a breeze. The jacket and beret were exerting a gentle pressure all their own. Nudging him toward the portal home, as his father said they would. They urged him to cross the street, to the side opposite from where the women and children had taken shelter. He ran.

A scream stopped him. He looked back toward the tank. A woman had apparently run across its path, toward the shelter. She was lying in the street, trying to push herself up with her arms. As David watched, she slumped and stopped moving.

He took a step back toward where the portal must be waiting. He could take no more of this. No more suffering, no more death. With a deep sadness, he realized what, besides death itself, they were risking in trying to rescue their mother. They would be witnesses to events that would change them forever.

He saw the woman in the street stir and felt a spark of hope. A toddler in a white dress pushed out from under the woman's arm. She stood and looked down at the woman, who must have been carrying her. She reached a small hand to the woman's blouse and tugged at it. Then, confused and frightened by the loud noises, the little girl tottered away.

Go, David thought. Then he said it out loud: "Go!"

The tank was rumbling toward her. It was thirty feet away, closing fast.

A French soldier shouted and ran toward her. A small barrel set into the front of the tank rattled, spitting flame. Bullets kicked up dirt at the man's feet. He dived and rolled under a partially crushed truck. Round after round plunked into the truck's sheet metal. The machine gun panned to the wall of rubble. It blasted the concrete into clouds of dust, keeping the fighters cowering behind.

David looked over his shoulder, down the side street he believed his beret would tumble into if he let it. The portal. It had to be close.

He ran . . . not toward the portal, but into the path of the tank. The machine gun kept spraying bullets at the fighters. He hoped the gunner would either not see him at all or would recognize his intention to get the little girl and that he would not mow him down. The turret and barrel of the big gun were still aimed off to one side. David was not sure the driver even knew what he was about to run over.

Fifteen feet. The metal treads rolled on, grinding cobblestones. The tank was five feet from the child when David snatched her up, reversed himself, and darted toward the nearest building.

He ducked inside and immediately knew he could not stay. It was the pub, with the burning bed falling through the ceiling. Most of the lower floor was now engulfed in flames. David and the little girl coughed in unison. She tried to cry but could only cough more wretchedly. David peered out at the tank. Soon it would be even with him and then past him. The German soldiers crowding behind it seemed to be looking for something to shoot.

Clutching the child to his chest, he rolled around the edge of the broken wall and back outside. Someone near the tank yelled at him. The language was different, harsher and scarier than the French he had heard earlier. He did not stop—did not *halt*, to use the word hurled at him. He stayed close to the buildings and hurried toward the French fighters, who had moved farther down the street. At a side street he stopped. Across the town's main road, beyond the first block of buildings, he saw the old men, women, and children from the shelter. They were pouring from a back door to escape the advancing army.

A hand gripped David's shoulder and pulled him backward. It was the Frenchman who had beckoned to him when he was standing in the street. The man eyed him from under a furled brow. "*Que faites-vous? Où appartenez-vous, fils?*"

David gaped at him. "Uh . . . uh . . ."

The man slung his rifle over a shoulder. He held his hands, rough and bleeding, out to the little girl.

David twisted away. At first the man appeared surprised; then a smile pushed at his stubbled cheeks. His eyes flicked to the little girl, and he said, "Marguerite." He nodded. "Marguerite."

She held a hand up to the man. David handed her to him.

The man whispered something soothing to the little girl. He trotted down the side street, away from the tank's approach. At the corner, he turned back to David. "*Venez, garçon!*" He gestured with his head for David to follow him.

David took several steps. When the man disappeared behind the building, David stopped. If his father was right, and he understood the meaning of the strange, subtle tugging from the jacket and beret, the portal home was in the burning building right beside him.

The tank was near. Another ten seconds and he would be in its sights again. A dozen paces away on the main street, bullets flew in both directions. He aimed himself at an open doorway and ran toward it. Its frame was on fire, but David raised his arms over his head and plunged through.

CHAPTER

Six

David burst into the antechamber as though he were falling down the stairs. He took a step and, not finding solid ground, fell to the floor on his stomach. As it had done when he ventured into the world of French resistance fighters and Nazi tanks, the air burst from his lungs. This time, however, he was able to pull it back in without any trouble. He heard the door slam behind him, and he rolled over to see it solidly shut. Smoke filled the room, and he realized it was coming from him. Flames danced on his sleeves, and he felt heat on his neck.

"Aaahhggg!"

He felt hands slapping at him. In a few seconds the fire was out. He cringed away until he recognized Xander and his father. They were calling his name, asking if he was all right.

Wind whipped around him, stirring the smoke and sand and whatever else from the other world had been clinging to him. The wind pulled all of it into the gap under the door and was gone.

All the fear he had pushed aside to survive the German onslaught rushed into his consciousness as fast and furiously as flames igniting gas fumes. Simultaneously, relief washed over him, dousing those flames even as they sparked to life. He squeezed his eyes shut and began to weep. He heard his father and brother's words, felt their hands stroking his hair, squeezing his shoulder. His breath hitched in and out as he let the tears flow.

He wasn't even sure why he was crying: Was it the death he had seen or that he had pulled free from its skeletal fingers? He remembered Xander's response coming back from the Colosseum, and his own—although it was less pronounced—when he'd come back from the jungle.

He wondered if their experiences with the portals were like extreme booster shots of powerful emotions, or if the crossing over itself somehow touched the emotional receptors in their brains. He had heard that surgeons could touch parts of the brain with electrical probes, causing the patient to feel emotions that had nothing to do with his current experiences or memory. He'd also heard that electrical shocks could force a person to lose control of his bathroom functions. He was really glad that hadn't happened to him. It made shedding a few tears less embarrassing.

"I'm all right, I'm all right," he said.

They were lifting him, setting him on the bench. He sniffed, rubbed his forearm across his eyes, under his nose.

"I'm all right."

"What happened?" Xander said. His face was right there, big worried eyes, trembling bottom lip. He had one hand pressed to David's back, the other on David's chest, as though he was still trying to grasp that David had returned . . . or making sure David didn't suddenly flutter away and zip out of the room through the crack under the door, like the other debris from the faraway world.

Dad had taken a step back. He had his arms crossed in front of him and was scowling at his younger son.

"I'm sorry," David said. "I thought . . . I thought I saw Mom."

"*Did* you?"

David bowed his head, thinking of his encounter with the woman in the room full of scared people. "No . . . it wasn't her."

"And you almost died, too, didn't you?" Dad snapped. His voice was hard, angry.

"Dad!" Xander said.

"He did! He almost died! David, am I wrong?"

David nodded his head. "You're right," he said weakly. "There was this battle . . . I was in some French town, I think. The Nazis were invading. I . . . I . . ." He shook his head.

"It's okay," Xander said. He was kneeling in front of David, still holding him, rubbing his back through the leather jacket.

David looked up at his father: *Is it okay?*

Dad held his stern composition, then softened under David's gaze. He skewed his mouth into a semi-smile. He stepped forward, knelt beside Xander, and leaned in to be close to David. His big hand engulfed David's shoulder.

"You scared me," he whispered. He blinked slowly, seeming to reselect his words. "I mean . . . I was scared for you."

David threw his arms around his father's neck. He thought he was going to cry again, but the tears didn't come. Instead, he felt Dad's warmth, his heart beating against his chest. He felt stronger, as though drawing energy from his father.

Dad said, "When I was a kid, I crossed over a few times without permission." He looked intently at David. "Twice I thought I saw my mother and, well . . . I did what you did. I just went."

David was grateful for Dad's telling him that. He knew how stupid he had been to just go. It was the kind of thing that would make his father take them all away from the house, regardless of Xander's determination to stay. It helped to know that Dad understood.

Then Dad pointed a stiff forefinger at David. "That

doesn't mean what you did is okay. It jeopardizes everything we're trying to do. If this is how it's going to be—"

"It's not!" David said. "I won't do that again. I promise."

Dad looked at Xander, who nodded. "Well," Dad said, "I think I'm going to put some locks on these doors, just in case."

"How are we going to find Mom?" Xander asked.

"That's the question, isn't it?" Dad said.

"We *are* going to find her," Xander said.

Dad squeezed his knee. "I said we would."

Xander stood. He slapped David on the leg. "Come on," he said. "We've got other rooms to check."

David's mouth dropped open. Did his brother really believe he was up to doing anything other than collapsing in a heap? Trying not to whine, he started, "Xan—"

"They can wait, Xander," Dad said. "Look at Dae. He's ready to fall over. We were up all night—Toria screaming about seeing the man in her room, then . . . Mom. And none of us has slept since then."

Xander said, "You crash. I'm going to find Mom."

Dad stepped close to him. "Xander, I know how you feel. But you have to bring it down a few notches. Your heart's probably beating a thousand times a minute. Your mind's racing. I know, I can see it in your eyes, in the way you're acting. Keep it up, and you won't be around long enough to find your mother."

Xander made an exasperated noise and started to turn away, but Dad grabbed his arm.

"I mean it," Dad said. "This isn't a sprint, Xander. It's a marathon. If we use up all our energy at the beginning, we won't cross the finish line. Pace yourself, son."

Xander looked ready to fight. Then David saw the wisdom of Dad's words reach his brother. Exhaustion and resignation washed over Xander like a sudden downpour. His shoulders slumped, his face slackened. He nodded and said, "Ready for bed, Dae?"

"Oh, man," David said. "Who needs a bed?"

CHAPTER

Seven

MOTHER OF MERCY NURSING HOME

LAKE FOREST, ILLINOIS

The old man's eyes snapped open. For a moment he did not know where he was. Then his surroundings came back to him: the pillow beneath his head, the thread of sunlight outlining the window where blackout blinds almost did their job, the *beep—beep—beep* of the machine that monitored his heartbeat. The beeps were coming fast as he sorted out what had woken him. It was not uncommon for him to lie awake all night, but his ninety-two years of living had earned him the right to doze when the day's brightness bothered his eyes. He could not remember the last time he had seen the midday sun, even what little of it seeped around the edges of the blinds.

What was it? he thought.

His eyes snapped back and forth as he separated dream-thoughts from memories, memories from false memories. No, not *false* memories: *changed* memories.

That's it!

The beeping picked up pace, rabbit quick now. The man tried to sort it out. *What* had changed? Dreams bumped into memories, memories shifted away. He was too old for this. Or was it simply that sleep was still whispering? Whispering mumbo jumbo in his ears. Was it that the change was too small to easily grasp, a shift in knowledge that affected others more than it ever had him? He scrunched his eyes shut, feeling the wrinkles of his face crowd together like the folds of a rumpled blanket. The beeping came loud and fast, and now he could feel his heart in his chest pounding, pounding.

It had been too long, decades since he'd sensed the change in memories, the shift in knowledge that he felt at that moment. It didn't matter *what* had changed, only that *something* had changed. All the implications of that added to his jumble of thoughts. Already crashing into themselves on the freeway of his mind.

It was coming to him, what it all meant.

The beeping was like an alarm now, urgent and demanding attention. He realized it *was* an alarm. His racing heart had crossed some threshold in the machine, which was screaming for help.

The door of his room burst open, and help ran in with clicking heels and wide eyes. The nurse ran to him and leaned her face close to his. He felt her hands gripping his shoulders, bony shoulders that had once been layered with heavy muscle.

"Mr. Wagner!" the nurse called, louder than was necessary. "Mr. Wagner!"

"They . . . they . . ." His voice was dry and thin, the vocal equivalent of a piece of straw. His hand came up and clutched at the nurse's uniform, her collar. He looked into her eyes, needing to share, needing to let someone else know.

"They've come back!" he said.

"Who?" the nurse asked.

She scanned the room, clearly not getting his meaning. How could she? He noticed that an unsure smile had found her lips and realized it was in response to his own shaky grin.

"They've come back," he repeated. It was not for her benefit anymore, but for his. He liked the sound of it. He liked what it meant.

He looked past the nurse, thinking, thinking. His smile fell away. Something else dawned on him.

"They don't know," he said. His eyes found the nurse's face again. He wanted desperately to communicate, to get this one thing across.

"What don't they know?" the nurse asked. She shook him gently. "Jesse, what don't they know?"

"The killer," the old man said. "He's still there. He doesn't want them in the house."

CHAPTER

SUNDAY, 9:01 A.M.

David had closed the curtains over their bedroom windows, but the room was still bright. Part of his mind screamed to hop up and do something: find Mom, make a plan, *something*.

The rest of him wanted nothing but sleep. His muscles felt heavy. When he closed his eyes, it felt as though he were sinking into his mattress—slowly, like quicksand. From time to time, all the things that had happened in the last few hours made his eyelids snap open. He'd notice the sunlight on the ceiling, the shadows of the leaves, and his lids would droop again. He started drifting, floating away on shadows as though on currents of water . . .

"David, you awake?"

His eyes sprang open. Back in his bedroom. Had Xander said something?

"Dae?"

He turned his head. Xander was on his own bed, his head propped up on his arm.

"How can you sleep?" Xander asked.

"I'm tired." The words came out as though his tongue were too big for his mouth.

"Mom's gone. We need to get her."

"We will," David said. He blinked slowly at his brother, some of what had been on his mind coming back. "We gotta work together. Stop fighting Dad."

"I'm not *fighting* him. It's just . . ." Xander dropped his head onto the pillow and spoke to the ceiling. "It's just that Dad and I have different ideas about how to get her back."

"Different how?"

"Like now. Look at us, in bed when we should be searching for her."

"Even soldiers sleep, Xander. I can't even think straight."

Each time his lids came down, David forced them open again, waiting for Xander to say something else. But he didn't.

His brother just kept staring up at the ceiling. Finally David's eyes closed, and he let them stay that way. Xander's breathing grew louder, more steady. David thought he heard a snore. And then he was out.

CHAPTER

nine

734 BC

OUTSIDE SIDON, ASSYRIAN EMPIRE

The assassin lost sight of his target. Smoke from the burning city behind him roiled in the sky like mud kicked up from the bottom of a pond. It blotted out the sun and cast shadows over the land. The assassin squinted at the last place he had seen the fleeing man and spotted him: There! *He was halfway to the distant mountain range, where the assassin knew the man hoped to find refuge in one of the many caves.*

The land between the two men was hard-packed earth, cracked like snake scales from a long season of drought and heat. Why his king wanted this barren country, the assassin did not know. But then, he was often commanded to kill for reasons known only to people more favored by the gods than he. His duty was to kill, not to ask questions. It was for this labor that he had been taken from his family on his eighth birthday and trained for over a dozen years. During this time, his abilities of stealth, resourcefulness and, he learned later, ruthlessness, set him apart from the other boys. So his masters had sent him away for special training under the tutelage of Gilgamesh, a man whose skills in the art of death were legendary. The assassin had discovered they were also very real.

He looked back at the crushed city. Against the shimmering blue backdrop of the Mediterranean Sea, the clay walls of its buildings rose out of the desert like a mirage.

From the city itself, smoke rose in columns like the blackened trees of a long-dead forest. The vast Assyrian army had pushed against the walls and poured into the streets. He was not part of that powerful force, though he worked to accomplish the same goals of protecting the empire and conquering new peoples and lands. If the army was a battering ram, he was a dagger. The army crushed whole cities, while he sliced at the few men who could rally those cities' legions or rebuild them from afar.

The prince he was after was just such a man.

The assassin had slipped into the city well ahead of the army. His task: to kill the king and his two grown sons. He had found the father and one son together, planning their response to the approaching invaders. Their deaths had been easy. The second son had been with his commanders, who had fought the assassin gallantly. In the end, the commanders had succumbed to the assassin's superior skills. Their efforts, however, had allowed the prince to escape.

The assassin's arrows had found the prince as he bolted away. But his own injuries had kept him from moving in for a quick kill.

He took a step and felt every one of those injuries. A heavy gash through a muscle in his thigh threatened to topple him. A puncture in his side, just under his ribs, made breathing difficult. He knew it needed attention, but he could not spare the time—not as long as the last prince drew breath. His forearms above the wide iron cuffs he wore for protection were bruised and cut, as was the back of his right hand. He tightened his grip on his knife, thankful to have not lost his hand's power and mobility.

Another step, and he did topple. His knees struck the dirt, as hard as tiles. He slouched down, needing to rest. His head felt like it was baking in his tight, cowhide cap. He pulled it off, letting his hair fall to his shoulders, over his eyes. He used the tip of his knife to flick it back off his face. He hitched in a breath and felt the wound in his side flare with white-hot pain. He tasted blood and spat it out. The reddish-pink glob evaporated on the scalding desert floor. He let his head roll back on his neck until he was staring up at the smoke-filled sky. There was no breeze to cool his skin, no water to quench his thirst. He closed his eyes.

He imagined himself as a king. Instead of blood, his fingers would be stained with wine. Instead of death, he would dream of life, the people of his empire stretching to the horizon, honoring him for letting them live.

His eyes snapped open, and he shook such imaginings out of his head.

It was not his destiny to wear gold, but to wield weapons. He did not have the power to grant life, only the duty to take it. To think otherwise would lead to weakness and insanity.

Gritting his teeth, gripping his knife, he forced himself to rise. His eyes found the prince, and his heart leapt with hope. The man appeared to be down, sprawled against the unkind earth. The sight put strength in his legs. He stumbled on, after his target.

When the assassin was fifty yards away, he saw the two arrows he had let fly. They were jutting from the prince's back. Their feathered ends swayed slightly, as though in a breeze. The assassin knew better: it was the prince's breathing that moved the arrows. His muscles tightened with determination to finish the job.

The prince stirred. His head lifted, and he pushed himself up onto his elbows. He turned and saw the assassin. His eyes flashed in terror. He got to his feet, every movement punctuated by a gasp of pain, a groan of effort. He lurched on toward the mountains.

The assassin let out a heavy sigh. Didn't the prince know it was over? Death was too near to hide from it any longer.

The man of death followed. He tried to pick up his pace, but his injuries were taking their toll.

On with it, *he thought.* End it now.

Ten minutes on, he figured he had closed the gap by only a few paces. He forced his legs to move faster. He switched the knife into his left hand, so his right could hold the wound in his thigh.

A scratch, *he told himself.* Is man defined by flesh and blood, or is he everything he has learned to be? I am an assassin because of my skills, my determination to perform well. My bones and sinew do not make me an assassin. My wounds cannot stop me from being one.

The sounds of the invasion behind him had faded. The smell of smoke had left his nostrils. A slight breeze swept down from the mountains, carrying the musty scents of eucalyptus and juniper. He was alarmed to realize how far they had walked from the city. There was no chance of the prince escaping, but he wondered if he himself would make it back before succumbing to his own injuries.

Great fissures came down from the foothills and carved jagged cracks into the desert floor. As the two men approached the first of these gashes in the earth, the assassin smiled. It was impossible to cross. The prince was as trapped by a rent in the ground as he would have been by a wall.

The prince stopped at the edge of the ten-foot-wide crevasse. He seemed to appraise it, then shifted his gaze back toward the assassin. With no other choice, he stepped forward and fell out of the assassin's view.

The assassin shook his head. Of course the man would not make this easy. He did not want to even think about having to climb back out of the fissure once he delivered the prince to Charon, Hades's ferryman.

At the edge, he looked down. The crevasse was barely deeper than a man, but no man lay at the bottom, as he had expected. He looked to the left and right, able to see a good distance in either direction. No one. No footprints. No blood. No deeper holes in which to hide. Directly below, something shimmered. He squinted at it. The light and shadows were playing tricks on him. Was that a pool of water? The entrance to a cavern? He couldn't tell, but something . . . something was there.

He stepped off the ledge to the first foothold. The dry ground crumbled under him. He slid down, tried to hold something, found nothing. He dug in his heels, skidded, and stopped.

He balanced on the edge of the pool, but it was no pool. The earth wavered at his feet. A mist stirred, obscuring whatever it was that caused the sight. He *crouched and passed his hand over the fog. It cleared, and his knifed hand shot up, ready to plunge down.*

There was the prince! Down in the pit—but he did not appear to be whole. To the assassin's eye, there was blood and body, not all together. An arm here. A torso there. Was it a trick of the air, the way it shimmered and moved? Or had an animal moved in on the prince?

A fast, silent animal, *the assassin thought.*

The assassin plunged his knife down. Coldness gripped his arm. It tugged at him. He tried to move back, but the earth under him gave way, and his feet went into the hole. More coldness, pulling . . . pulling. With one arm and both feet ensnarled by this trap, he knew he was going in.

He raised his face to the sky and yelled—not in fear, but in defiance and effort: He would not die easily. Whatever pulled him would feel his blade, his teeth, his determination.

Then, in a flash, he went in.

And vanished.

CHAPTER

SUNDAY, 3:33 P.M.

Sitting on the front porch steps, David bounced his soccer ball on a lower step between his legs. He had planned on practicing his dribbling and making some shots into a makeshift goal while waiting for Dad and Toria to return from the hardware store, but he didn't feel like it now. He squinted up at the sun through the trees. His eyes were achy, and he felt groggy and ready for bed, even though it was midafternoon.

"Not used to sleeping during the day," he said.

"Sleep's sleep," Xander said.

David lowered his eyes to find his brother, but saw only his own ghostly image reflected in the lens of Xander's camcorder. Xander paced in front of him, pulling in and out with the camera. Stooping almost to the ground to get weird—Xander would say *artistic*—angles.

"Quit stalling," Xander said. "What happened in that World War II village you went to this morning?"

"I don't want to talk about it."

"Just a little," Xander coaxed. "We've gotta document what we're doing here."

"Why?"

"Come on, Dae. How many people can say they rescued their mother from time-traveling thugs?"

"We haven't found her yet."

"We will, and we'll have the story of it on tape. We'll be millionaires, I'm telling you."

"Are you filming my sneaker?" David kicked at the camera, connecting with it harder than he had intended.

"Hey!" Xander yelled. He turned the camera to look at the lens. "You're going to break it, and you almost jabbed it through my eye."

David just frowned at him. He had sat through Xander's walking completely around him, filming and saying things like, "This is the boy who fought off a Nazi tank" and "Ladies and gentlemen: the wound." Here Xander zoomed in on the place where David's hair had been singed at the back of his neck and the collar of his shirt had caught fire. He hadn't been burned, and there was no wound.

Then Xander had started asking questions about his time in the French village, and David had realized that it wasn't such a fun memory. He hadn't found his mother as he thought he would, he was almost killed, and death and terror had been all around him. It wasn't just this last jaunt to World War II that bothered him.

"I know I was all gung ho about checking out these worlds. I mean, I insisted on going into that jungle where the tigers almost got me. And when I thought I saw Mom, I just went. But, I don't know . . ." He shook his head. "I'm starting to think there's nothing good about those worlds. It's just death . . . and danger."

Xander said, "We gotta find Mom, Dae."

"That makes it so much worse, that we *have* to go through."

He examined his brother's face, looking for any sign that he was as worried and reluctant as David. But Xander's expression was unreadable. Since Mom's kidnapping, Xander's determination to find her made all of his emotions—anger at Dad, sadness for Mom—look the same.

David said, "After you came back from the Colosseum, you didn't ever want to see those doors again. Aren't you still afraid of what's on the other side?"

"Of course I am."

"You don't act like it."

"We gotta find Mom," Xander repeated. "That's all that matters. That's all I think about."

"But you're out here with your camera, talking about making a documentary. We're getting ready for school tomorrow. Mom can't be all you're thinking about."

Xander sat on a lower step and twisted to look up at David. "I've been thinking about what Dad said, that our best chance to find her is if we have all the time we need to do it and none of us gets hurt. I want to find her today, *right now*, but what if it takes longer—a month or even a year? We can't have people curious about what we're doing, why we're not in school, why we've become recluses. We need to look like a normal family."

"Even if we're not," David added with a half smile.

"*Especially* because we're not," Xander said. "People will leave us alone if they think there's nothing special about us. And Dad needs to make money. We need to live, eat. We might need to buy things to help in the search."

David thought about that. "Like what?"

Xander shrugged. "Like rope," he said, unsure. "Like the locks Dad's getting now. There's always something. I've seen movies where people lost wars because they couldn't afford to keep fighting. If we want to keep looking for as long as it takes, we need money, and that means Dad has to work."

David pictured Dad going into his office at the school, listening to parents complain, disciplining students, hiring teachers . . . whatever else principals did. He imagined himself grinning at teachers, raising his hand to answer a question, making new friends. All with Mom gone—*kidnapped.* "I don't think I can do it," he said. "Just pretend everything's okay?"

Xander set the camcorder on a step and gripped David's knee. "I don't want to either. I wanna be up there now, going through every door, but that would be like jumping in the ocean to rescue a friend when you can't swim. You both end up dead. Better to find a lifeguard or throw in a life preserver. That's how Dad wants to handle it: smart and safe." He smiled. "So be the gloomy kid, if you have to. Just don't be the weirdo who never showers and always rambles about living in a haunted house."

David said, "It *is* haunted . . . in a way."

"Sort of," Xander agreed. His eyes took in the front doors. "The past lives here, doesn't it? I mean, *really.*"

"I wish it didn't," David said. "And I wish we didn't have to keep visiting it."

"Maybe we'll find Mom right away."

"You think so?" David asked.

Xander didn't answer. He didn't have to.

They heard the SUV's engine and its tires crunching over the dirt road, and turned their heads to wait for its appearance around the bend. The sun flashed brightly off its hood and windshield, reminding David that it was a sunny world away from the woods in which they lived. The 4Runner swung around and stopped at the end of the road.

Toria climbed out and waved. She waited for Dad to come

around from the other side. She took one of three heavy-looking plastic bags from him, and the two of them trudged into the forest toward the boys.

"Been out here the whole time?" Dad asked.

"You told us to," Xander said, a little whine in his voice.

Dad's eyes roamed the front of the house as he approached. It seemed to David that he was expecting to see something he hoped he wouldn't. When Dad was close enough, David tossed him the ball.

Dad grabbed for it, but the bags hindered his dexterity, and he knocked the ball into the trees. He shrugged and hefted the bags. "I'll feel better once we have these locks on the doors." He looked from David to Xander and frowned.

David thought he was going to comment on the mopey expression on Xander's face, which he was sure matched his own. But Dad simply shared their sadness. How could they feel any other way?

He set the bags at the base of the stairs and sighed. He said, "Come on, all of you. I want to show you something."

"What?" David said.

Dad began walking toward the side of the house. "You'll see."

The kids threw puzzled looks at each other. Then Xander pushed off the steps to follow. Toria dropped her bag with the others and fell in behind him. David considered staying right where he was. He'd seen enough for that day . . . for that *year*. But curiosity got the better of him. He jumped down to the ground and hustled to catch up.

eleven

SUNDAY, 3:50 P.M.

Dad led David, Xander, and Toria to the clearing. It was way behind the house, through an especially dense area of forest. David and Xander had been there before, and its strangeness came back to David as soon as he stepped into it. It was an almost perfect oval carved out of the woods. The ground here was flat and grassy. The tall trees around it bent in, forming what looked to him like a naturally domed arena. Stranger than its physical appearance was the way it affected people: it made David's stomach feel funny, like plunging a long way down in an elevator; it seemed to allow them to run slightly faster than normal; and it caused their voices to be higher pitched, as though they were talking with their lungs filled with helium.

Everyone but David stopped at the edge of the clearing. He continued toward its center. He said, "Dad, we already know about this place. Remember, you found us here the other day?"

As he walked farther into the clearing, his voice rose in pitch until "the other day" was as squeaky as Mickey Mouse's. Despite the sour mood he had carried with him from the porch steps to the clearing, he laughed. It came out like a little girl's giggle. That got him laughing harder, which made his voice seem even more distorted and ridiculous.

The others began laughing as well, but at the edge of the clearing their voices sounded normal. Xander laughed so hard, tears streamed down his face, and he fell to his knees.

Toria managed to say, "Why are you . . . why are you talking like that?"

David beckoned her to him. "Come here!" he squeaked.

When she was near, she said, "What?"—as high-pitched as a rusty hinge. Her eyes went wide, and her hand flew up to cover her mouth.

David cracked up again.

"Was that me?" Toria squealed.

Xander rose and walked into the clearing, wiping at his face.

"Dad," he said. The last part of the word was higher pitched than the first. "Dad. What's this about? Do you know?"

Dad shook his head and joined them. "I know what this clearing *does*, but not why." Even his deep voice was no match for the squeakifying power of the clearing.

"Is this why you brought us here?" Xander asked. "For a . . . I don't know, a *break* from the doom and gloom?"

"It worked," David said. "I've been frowning so much, my face hurts."

It was about four in the afternoon. He could not believe that his mother had been gone for only twelve hours. He knew he shouldn't feel as lighthearted as he did, but he couldn't help it. He wondered if the laughing gas some dentists used had the same effect: making you feel like laughing when you should be crying.

David smiled at Toria. She was holding her arms out from her body and rising up on her tiptoes and down again, rising up . . . she was feeling the lightness, the *bounciness* David and Xander had noticed the first time they were here.

Dad said, "This isn't the half of it, guys. Watch." He moved deeper into the clearing and stopped near its center. He faced them, but his attention was on something they couldn't see. He looked around as though tracking a flying insect. Holding his hands out, seemingly for balance, he rocked up onto his toes. He took a step, rocked up again.

Xander and David exchanged a look of complete bafflement.

"Hold on!" Dad squeaked. His foot rose high, but instead of coming back down, the rest of him rose up to its level.

David gasped. Toria made a noise that might have been a startled scream. Xander spat out a word: "*What?*"

It was as though their father was standing on an invisible platform—an unstable platform. His feet wobbled around beneath him. He kept shifting his knees, his weight whipping his arms this way and that, apparently to keep from falling. Instead of coming down, he slid sideways and rose higher. Still wobbling, his eyes came off his feet to take in his startled children. A wide grin stretched across his face. His hair rose and fell as though blown by a breeze. He said, "What do you think?" The act of speaking seemed to distract him from whatever concentration he needed to—

To what? David thought. *Fly? Float?* The way Dad was balancing himself, David would say Dad was grinding a rail on a skateboard.

Dad wobbled and went higher.

"You've got to be kidding me!" Xander said, stepping forward. "Are you . . . are you *flying?*"

"I don't know what it is," Dad said. He shifted his hips, moved sideways and up.

Correction, David thought. *Not grinding a rail—more like riding an escalator. An invisible escalator that isn't very stable.*

The smile never left Dad's face. He said, "We discovered this when I was a kid. There are like . . . air currents or something. But more than air. If you find them, you can kind of step on them, *ride* them." He suddenly sailed thirty feet through the air, going sideways, straight up, then plunging down a little. His body wobbled as he tried to stay balanced. He let out a long, high "Aaaah!" and laughed. "Not so much a ride as it is like *surfing* on whatever currents are moving through this clearing."

David stuck out his foot, feeling for something he could not see, hoping to feel it. Nothing, just that same lightness everywhere. He called, "How? Can we do it too?"

"Sure you can!" Dad said. He zipped higher and came closer to the kids. He hovered over them, smiling down at David.

David could see the bottoms of his shoes, a spot of gum stuck on one of them. For some reason, this more than anything drove the point home: his dad was flying. And he seemed to be getting more comfortable in the air, less wobbly, more in control.

Their father shot backwards and stopped. He was still looking down at David, but not between his feet. He said, "It has something to do with attitude, with *wanting* to do it. It's like flexing a muscle to find the currents. I'm not saying you're willing yourself to do it—more like you're *allowing* yourself to do it."

David lifted his foot again, tapping his toe in the air. He *did* feel something, a kind of resistance. He moved his whole foot. The air felt spongy, as though he were stepping on a balloon. He heaved himself up onto it and came straight down. He lost his balance and fell back onto the ground.

Xander and Toria laughed.

From high above, Dad called, "That's it, Dae! You can do it. It takes some getting used to."

David leaned back on his arms to look up at Dad, and he realized something. "You did this before," he said to his father. "I mean recently. When you found Xander and me here the other day, you'd been doing this, huh?" He remembered that Dad had been out of breath, his hair all messed up.

Dad shrugged. He zipped around in a tight circle, rose even higher, close to the level of the treetops now. "I confess," he said, and laughed. "I wondered if the clearing still allowed it and if I could do it. After you guys found the portals, and Xander went to the Colosseum, I needed a break. This place takes your mind off everything."

David lay back, feeling the soft grass under him, tickling the back of his neck. The trees arched over the edges of the clearing, leaving an oval of blue sky directly above. Nothing indicated that the imaginary dome created by mentally extending the treetops to the center of the opening was the highest you could go, but he suspected that was true. His father was just below this upper limit, weaving around. Instead of standing straight, he was starting to lean over. This made what he was doing appear even more like flying.

"Whoa! David, look!"

It was Xander. When David looked, his brother was standing four feet above the grass.

CHAPTER

twelve

SUNDAY, 4:12 P.M.

Xander laughed. His feet, well off the ground, were slipping and sliding around under him, but he somehow stayed up.

"Check it out!" Xander yelled.

"Oh, man," David said, getting to his feet. If Xander could do it, he'd better be able to. He walked to the center of the clearing, thinking that the currents, whatever they were, would be stronger there. Toria was closer to the edge. She was lifting her feet and hopping, but not getting any air.

She'd better not do it before me, David thought.

He closed his eyes and patted the air around him. After a moment he felt the resistance he had noticed earlier. Again, he lifted his foot and moved it around, as though feeling for a stair. More resistance, but nothing else.

Come on, come on! he thought. *Fly!*

Sponginess under his feet, under his hands. Squeezing his eyelids tighter, he imagined the air holding him, lifting him.

"David!" Xander called.

David looked.

Xander was *way* above ground now, grinning like a madman. "Yeah, man!"

David felt his feet almost slip out from under him, as though he were standing on ice. At the same time, he realized he was not looking up at Xander. He dropped his gaze straight down and saw the grass ten feet below his shoes. His stomach rolled. His muscles tightened. His feet *did* slip out from under him. He fell back, his arms pinwheeling, his legs shooting up over his head. But he didn't drop. He saw the ground below him and then Xander again as he came back around. He had done a backward somersault in midair.

"Way to go, Dae!" Xander said. He threw himself backward. He spun his arms and kicked his feet until he had executed a similar move.

David watched with amazement. He felt pressure under his feet and arms, as though invisible hands were keeping him afloat.

He brought his arms down and kicked as he would under-water. And what would happen underwater happened here: he rose higher. As frightening as it was to watch the ground get farther away, David felt a lightness that went deeper than his skin and muscles. It reached his spirit. It was like he was free of more than the laws of gravity; all the garbage that had been dumped on him recently didn't seem so heavy.

He was still aware of his mother's absence and how awful it was. But at this moment, he felt able to deal with it. He was sure it was temporary, as though she had gone to the store and would return soon. He laughed at that, kicked his legs, and shot higher. Bending at the waist, he leaned diagonally over the ground. This—staring directly at a forty-foot plunge—was even more exhilarating. His heart raced faster. His mouth twitched from a joyful smile to a worried frown and back again. His father called to him, and when he turned to look, his body rotated with his head.

Dad was standing—if that's what you called it, when there was nothing to stand on—as high as David thought he could go, at the center of the opening to the wide blue sky.

"What do you think?" Dad said and laughed.

David meant to answer, but only an excited breath came out. He swallowed and tried again. "Great!"

Just under the arcing canopy of leaves, Xander hovered. He

was reaching up to touch the branches. He was being careful, as though any connection with reality would send him crashing back down.

"I can't do it!"

Toria's voice reached David, sounding thin and far away. He looked to see her jumping in place on the grass.

Dad said, "I think you're trying too hard, honey." He moved his arms and legs and began descending toward her.

David swiveled away and "swam" toward the canopy at the edge of the clearing. How cool would it be to get a leaf from up here and save it as a memento of his first time flying? He still had trouble thinking of it as *flying*. It wasn't like *Peter Pan*: hadn't Wendy, John, and Michael Darling needed fairy dust? And they had flown away to Neverland.

David, Xander, and Dad weren't flying, and they would never go anywhere this way. But that was all right. This was enough.

He was near the edge of the clearing and reaching up to a leaf bigger than his hand, when something outside the clearing caught his eye. His eyes widened, and his heart felt squeezed into a tight knot. Through the trees, on the ground, a man stood looking at him. He was in shadows, but David could tell the man's expression was grim. He had long hair that was blowing around his head. He wore a dark overcoat, and his hands were stuffed into his pockets. The whites of his eyes seemed to glow in the darkness of the woods.

David hitched in a breath and tried to yell for Dad, but his mind would not form the words he wanted to use. He moved his mouth without saying a thing.

He suddenly realized he was still moving, fast and out of control. He saw a heavy tree branch seconds before he crashed into it. His face hit first, then his chest. The pressure or currents that had been holding him up suddenly evaporated, and he fell.

His hands clawed for the trees and grabbed a branch. His descent jerked to a stop, then the branch snapped and he kept falling. His fingers tore at leaves and twigs. Like a freight train, the ground rushed at him.

David screamed.

CHAPTER

thirteen

The assassin tumbled over the body of the prince. He realized instantly that the man was intact; it must have been a trick of the light, the shimmering, that had made him think the prince had been torn apart.

The assassin crashed down against a wood-planked floor. His ankle twisted; the puncture in his side flared with fresh pain. He ignored it. Instead, he rolled away from his adversary, away from any slicing blades the injured man might swing at him. A wall stopped him short. So he twisted and spun and plunged his knife into the prince's back, cracking through the left shoulder blade to reach the heart. The prince did not utter a gasp of death. He did not spasm in a final effort to retain life. The man had been dead before the assassin's knife—from the arrows, surely. But the assassin was trained to consider all possibilities before a normal person would think of even one. Could someone else have killed him, someone now hiding?

He looked around. He was in a small room with doors on opposite walls. A wooden bench, some items hanging on the wall above the bench—a helmet, tunic, an archer's bow. One door was open, revealing the walls of the crevasse into which he had jumped in search of the prince. Beyond the crevasse, black smoke streaked through a blue sky.

The door slammed shut. The assassin leaped for it. He tugged and pushed at a circular metal protrusion, but the door did not budge. Light glowed from a torch mounted on the ceiling, but it did not flicker with flames, and when he held his palm up to it, the light did not warm it. He squinted suspiciously.

A banging noise came from the other door. Quickly, he pressed his foot against the back of the prince and extracted his knife. He swung it toward the door, crouching, ready to spring. With no place to hide, he would simply have to fight whatever confronted him.

The banging continued, and he realized it was not coming from the door itself, but somewhere beyond. He stepped silently to the door and listened.

Bang, bang, bang.

It was not at this door that someone pounded. Perhaps, he thought, the people here knew an intruder had entered their midst. Maybe this banging was an alarm.

He must have stumbled into secret caves the Sidonians used to escape from their enemies. But why would they have put so much effort into the construction of a subterranean hideaway? *The room was a perfect box, its walls smoother than he had ever seen outside of a king's palace.* That's it, he thought, *this place must be a sanctuary for Sidon's nobility. That's why the prince, and not commoners, had fled to it. Only a select few knew of it.*

Bang, bang.

And one of them was beyond the door, obviously deeper into the cave. He put his fingers on the metal knob and pulled. The door remained shut, as he had expected it would. Like the other door, its latch was hidden. Then his hand moved, and the knob turned with it. He heard a click, and the slab of door came loose from the wall. He inched it open and peered through the crack. He saw a corridor stretching out of sight. It was narrow, as a tunnel should be. Like the room, however, the walls had been carved smooth and shaped into a rectangle. Fifteen feet away, a man studied the frame of another door on the other side of the corridor. While the assassin watched, the man slammed a tool into it: bang, bang.

What would he be doing at a time like this? Certainly, he knows about the city's besiegement.

But the man's relaxed posture and casual movements indicated no knowledge of the war outside or of the assassin's intrusion.

Good, *the assassin thought,* the man will be dead before he realizes his ignorance.

At that moment the first door blew open. Blinding light flooded in, along with a wind that carried stinging grains of sand and swirling smoke. The wind whipped through the small room and back out the door from which it came, like a genie's invisible hand reaching for the assassin. He squinted against the light and the blowing sand, and his hair flapped like a flag pointing at the wide-open door.

When he looked, the man in the corridor was staring back at him. The wind pulled the door out of his hand, opening it all the way. The wind was pulling everything. The hem of his chiton, which hung from belt to mid-thigh, snapped up and down and then pulled tight toward the open door. He thought again of a hand tugging at him.

The body of the prince began sliding along the floor. The shafts of the arrows extending from his back bowed in the fierce wind. A gust howled in and, as it departed, took the prince's body with it. The assassin watched the prince fly through the door and vanish in the light. The wind pulled at the assassin's feet, and he fell. His knife was ripped from his hand. It disappeared into the bright void beyond the threshold. The assassin would have gone through next, had he not gripped the frame of the other doorway.

The man in the corridor rushed toward him, his expression changing from bafflement to alarm.

The assassin was powerless to defend himself. It was all he could do to hold on to the frame and resist the force that pulled at him. Everything in him screamed out against being taken through that other door. Before the wind had come, he had seen the crevasse and smoke-filled sky on the other side. Now there was nothing but light and wind. Perhaps his nation had angered the gods by attacking this land. Or maybe he had stumbled into the lair of some beast unknown to his people. At that moment all he knew was that he must not go back through that door.

He pulled with all his might toward the hall, but the wind's grip on him was too strong. The other man reached him, grabbing for his arms. He seemed suddenly to become aware of the storm. He lurched forward, and the assassin thought this man, too, was going to fly right past him and out the door. But the man jammed his feet into the corridor wall on either side of the door's frame. Over the howl of the wind the assassin could hear the man yelling in a strange tongue. The man held firmly to the assassin's arms.

The assassin noticed the man's clothes and hair were flapping only slightly and realized the pull of the wind was not as fierce outside the small room. He had to get out. Seeking to gain more leverage, he released one hand from the door frame and gripped the man's clothes under his neck. The man canted his body backward, pulling the assassin with him.

The wind grew even stronger. The assassin's sandals came apart and flew away—first one, then the other. Near panic now, he tugged hard on the man in the corridor, putting him off balance. The man flipped forward, over the assassin and into the blinding light beyond the other door. The assassin squinted back, watching the man disappear. As soon as he vanished, the door slammed shut, and the wind died.

The assassin gripped the door frame and kept his eyes on the closed door for a long time. When it didn't burst open again, he pulled himself into the corridor, rolled away from the room, and stared up at the ceiling until his breathing and his heartbeat slowed to normal. Finally he sat up. The corridor was dimly lit from vessels of light attached to the walls. Like the light in the ceiling of the small room, they did not flicker with flame. Everything about this place was strange.

He nodded to himself. He had thought a beast resided here. The strangeness seemed to confirm that suspicion.

Grunting, feeling his wounds and aching muscles, the assassin stood. With the caution and stealth that was as natural to him as breathing, he approached the open doorway to the little room. It was cleared of everything he and the prince had brought into it: no sand, no weapons, no clothes. Even the blood they had shed was gone.

Strangely—but no stranger than the rest of this place—the items still hung from hooks over the bench. He remembered them rattling against the wall as the wind tugged at them, and he wondered how they survived its devastating pull.

He stepped into the room, just far enough to reach his fingers around the edge of the door. He pulled it shut as he backed into the corridor and stood quietly. He kept his eye on the door, expecting something to lurch out at him. His ears, accustomed to hearing the slightest scrape or breath, sensed nothing. He scanned the corridor one way and then the other, and the skin on the back of his neck tightened as he realized that the door he had just shut was only one of many. Who knew what monsters lurked behind the others? If they were anything like the wind-beast he had survived, he was in no hurry to meet them. A wall blocked one end of the corridor. Set into the other end was an opening. Shadows lay beyond. He was used to darkness. He thrived in it. He walked toward it. Leaning against the walls for support, he stumbled past the doors, determined to find a way out of this labyrinth of ghosts and monsters.

CHAPTER

fourteen

David sat on a treatment table in the Pinedale Community
Health Clinic. Every time he shifted his weight, paper crinkled
under him. He frowned at the newly plastered cast encasing
his left arm. A nurse had given him pills for the pain, but it
still felt like someone was twisting the point of a knife into
his forearm. Dad ran his fingers over David's head, sweeping
the hair off his face.

David wrinkled his nose at him. "It still hurts," he said.

Dad brushed his fingers over David's cheek. "I'm sorry. Nothing like that ever happened to me, just falling like that."

"I lost my concentration. That man . . ."

David had already told his father about the man he had seen in the woods. While Dad was checking him for more injuries and scooping him up to carry him to the car, Xander had run into the woods for a look. By the time Dad pushed through the dense vegetation surrounding the clearing, David in his arms, Toria holding on to his pants pocket, Xander had returned. He had not spotted anyone or seen any signs that someone had been there.

"But he was there! I saw him!" David had insisted. He had not wanted his father to think that the excitement of flying had caused him to be reckless. Plus, Dad should know that somebody had been there. Somebody had *seen* them.

Dad had given him a squeeze and said, "Let's not worry about him right now, Dae."

That had made him feel better, but now that he knew he was going to be all right, the man's presence concerned him again.

"You're sure he saw you?" Dad whispered.

David nodded. "He was looking right at me. Just standing there."

"You've never seen him before?

David thought about it. "I don't think so."

"Long, dark hair? How old?"

"His face was in shadows, but I think he was old . . . older than you."

"Wow, he must've been ancient."

David smiled. "Sorry."

Dad stroked David's head again. He said nothing.

David looked up at him. "What does it mean, someone seeing us like that? I mean . . . it can't be good, right?"

Dad frowned. "I don't know." He leaned closer to whisper. "David, you're sure he wasn't the same man who . . . the one who took Mom?"

David shook his head. "No way. The guy who took Mom was bald and *big*. The guy in the woods was a lot skinnier. The one who . . . who . . ."

As soon as Dad had mentioned Mom, David felt his chest tighten. His eyes stung with unreleased tears. Getting hurt bad enough to go to the emergency room was just the kind of thing that brought out the best in his mother. She would be here comforting him, assuring him that everything would be all right. Dad had been there for him, saying the right things, coming to his rescue. But he wasn't Mom.

When he'd fallen, and all the way to the clinic, David had yelled and groaned. He had gritted his teeth and essentially handled the scariness of the fall, the pain of his arm, and his concern over having been seen. Now, with the thought of Mom thrown into the mix, it was more than he could bear. His father's face swam out of focus as tears filled David's eyes. He lowered his head, and fat drops fell onto the hospital gown covering his lap.

Dad pulled him close and hugged him. The paper under him crinkled again. It reminded him that he was in a strange place—not just the hospital, but Pinedale and the house itself. They were away from everything and everyone they knew, and bad things had happened. He wanted to go home, to his bedroom in Pasadena, to the familiar walls and smells and faces that would come to smile at him and wish him well.

He hitched in a breath. "I . . . I . . ." He let the tears come. Then he caught his breath and tried again: "I don't like it here. I want to go home."

"I know," his father said, pulling him closer. David took some comfort from Dad's big hand on his head.

He sniffed. "I want Mom!"

"Me too," Dad said. "We'll get her, Dae. We'll—"

"Mr. King?"

Shiny black shoes came back into David's view. David didn't want to look up at the doctor, not with his face all wet and his nose running. He sniffed again and told himself to stop with the waterworks.

"Is he still in pain?" the doctor asked.

Dad rubbed David's back. He said, "I think the scare of falling out of the tree caught up with him."

"Are you all right, David?" the doctor asked.

His voice was smooth and calm. David wondered how

many times a day he used those words. David nodded, then sniffed again. He wiped at his face with his fingers.

The doctor stepped away. He returned, holding a handful of tissues where David could see them.

"Mr. King, could we speak in private a moment?"

"Of course."

The doctor's shoes clicked against the tiles as they left the room.

Dad leaned close to David, gave him another squeeze. He whispered, "I'll be right back."

He wiped his face and looked up to watch his father step into the hallway, look both directions, then step off to the right.

He wondered what the doctor needed to say in private?

David slid off the table, cringing at the crinkling paper, ignoring the throbbing of his arm. The nurse had helped him remove his shirt—taking extra care to slip it off his injured arm—and given him the gown. He still wore his own pants and sneakers, which was a good thing now: he knew how to walk quietly in them. He crept to the open door and listened. Dad and the doctor were talking in the hall. Their voices were hushed, but David could make out the words.

Doctor: " . . . just asking if everything is okay at home."

Dad: "And I'm asking what that has to do with my son falling out of a tree."

Doctor: "I know that's what you said happened, but—"

Dad, his voice getting louder: "What do you mean, *I said*?"

Doctor: "The boy has other injuries, older, not consistent—"

Dad: "What injuries?"

Doctor: "Mr. King . . . he has a scabbed-over cut on his shoulder."

Boy, these guys catch everything, David thought. He had completely forgotten that the tribesmen had shot arrows at him when he'd gone into the jungle world. The three tigers that had wanted him for dinner had made the armed men seem like nothing big. But one of their arrows had cut his shoulder.

Doctor: "He has a black eye, a bruise on his cheek. It looks like—"

Dad: "Like *what*? What are you saying?"

Doctor: "I just want to make sure David is safe."

Dad: "From what? From *whom*? Are you suggesting that someone at home is hurting him? That *I'm* hurting him?"

Doctor: "I'm simply—"

David stormed into the hallway. The doctor's eyes grew big at something he saw in David's face, and he tried to smile.

"You think what you want," David said, his voice loud against the tiles and smooth walls. "My dad loves me and has never hurt me!"

He stopped beside his father, who put his hand on his shoulder. "It's okay, Dae."

"No, it's not," David said. He never took his eyes off the doctor. "We came here for help, and you just accuse my dad of something . . . something . . . *horrible.*" Folding his cast close to his body, he pointed at his bruised cheek with his other hand. "For your information, my brother did this. We were playing, and it got a little rough, okay?" David threw a glance up and down the hallway, but Toria and Xander had wandered somewhere else. "He's around here somewhere. You should see *his* head."

Dad stepped between him and the doctor. He gave David a look that was both stern and compassionate. He said, "That's enough, David, I can handle this."

"But—"

"I got it," Dad said. "Really."

David opened his mouth to continue, then pressed his lips together, sealing his words inside.

Dad smiled at him—the same smile that had comforted David many times: when David had not made the top-ranked soccer team, whenever nightmares had awakened him. He realized that he had been wrong before. They had not left *everything* familiar behind. They still had each other.

Dad turned back to the doctor. "Are we done here?"

"I just . . ." The doctor seemed to change his mind about what he wanted to say. "The nurse will get David a sling, and you'll be all set. We'll need to see him back here in a week."

Like everything is normal, David thought. *Like you didn't just accuse Dad of beating his kids.*

"Thank you," Dad said, playing the game as well. He turned David's shoulder to lead him back to the room.

David gave the doctor his fiercest scowl.

He hoped the man felt ashamed, but he just nodded at David and turned away.

CHAPTER

fifteen

SUNDAY, 6:20 P.M.

In the car on the way home, David was still brooding. He was
in the front passenger seat. Toria sat in the back with Xander,
complaining that all Xander had done at the hospital was sit
in the waiting room and text his friends. Even now, he was
clicking away on his cell phone.

Dad moved the rearview mirror to see his elder son. He asked,
"Is that Dean you're text messaging, Xander? How is he?"

Xander shook his head. "It's Danielle."

"So how is *she*?"

Xander's thumbs tapped out a message. He let out a disgusted sigh, flipped the phone closed, and dropped it onto the seat beside him.

"Problem?" Dad asked.

"*Girls*," Xander said. He crossed his arms and glared out the window.

When he didn't continue, Dad said, "Is she giving you a hard time for moving?"

"It's not that. Just . . . I don't know. She's being nice, I guess."

"But . . . ?"

"But she's acting like we didn't spend almost every minute together this summer. She says the weather's been nice. She saw the new Matt Damon movie last weekend. Chitchat."

Dad nodded. He caught David's eye and raised his eyebrows in a *what's-a-guy-to-do?* way.

The sling the nurse had given David was blue and took the weight of the cast off his arm. The white plaster extended from his elbow to his hand, where it covered his palm and ran between his thumb and forefinger. He doubted he was ever going to get used to it.

"Can I sign your cast?" Toria chimed from behind him.

"I didn't like that guy," David told his father.

Dad gave him a puzzled look. "Who?"

"That doctor, what he was saying."

"What'd he say?" Xander asked. He sounded glad to shift his thoughts away from his ex-girlfriend.

"I wanna sign it," Toria repeated, louder.

"He didn't mean anything by it," Dad said. "It's his job to look out for his patients, especially children."

"You didn't seem too happy about it."

Dad shrugged. "He caught me off guard."

Xander said, "What? What'd he say?"

David twisted in the seat, bumping his injured arm and sending a bolt of pain into his shoulder. His words came out sounding angrier than he intended. "The doctor practically accused Dad of beating me."

"He said Dad *broke your arm?*" Xander's eyes grew wide in disbelief.

David said, "We told him I fell out of a tree, and he said, 'So you say.' He asked if everything was okay at home and how I got this bruise on my face."

Xander was leaning forward as far as the seat belt would let him. "What did you say?"

David smiled. "That you did it."

"Well," Xander said, sizing up the bruise, "it is in the shape of a fist."

Now David's cheek was starting to ache, just thinking about how the man who had taken Mom had punched him. He touched his fingers gently to his face. He said, "Yeah, but about twice the size of *your* fist."

"Okay, then," Dad said, "can you blame the doctor for asking?"

David scrunched his face at him. "But, Dad, come on! You beating us?"

Dad frowned. "It happens, guys. Not everyone should be a parent."

They rode in silence for a minute.

Finally Dad said, "This is the kind of thing we have to anticipate. We've got injuries we can't explain . . . your mother's absence . . ."

"*Flying!*" David said, dramatically.

"We can't do much about what people actually see," Dad said. "But, David, when we told the doctor you fell out of a tree and you said Xander had caused the bruise on your face, those were lies."

"What else was I supposed to say?"

Dad held up his hand. "I know, I know. What I'm saying is . . ." He paused, struggling with his words. "It's just that . . . I think we're going to have to get used to lying for a while."

Toria gasped. "Daddy!"

"Just for a while," Dad said. "If we tell the truth about Mom and everything else, they'll either think we're crazy and lock us up, or think that we're hiding something and start an investigation."

"We *are* hiding something," Toria said.

Dad glanced back at her. "They'll think we hurt Mom."

"Like they think you hurt me," David said.

Dad nodded. "The truth is too weird."

"We can show them," Toria suggested.

"Oh, yeah!" Xander said. "The government would move in and take the house. Then we'd never find Mom."

Dad turned the SUV onto the narrow dirt road that ended at their property. He said, "We have a secret. Sometimes you have to lie to keep secrets safe."

"*You* know all about that," Xander said.

"Xander!" David snapped. It would be a long time before his brother forgave Dad for bringing all of them to the house in the first place. He was about to say something else, something about letting it go, when Dad spoke up.

"You're right, Xander, I do. And I regret it. But until we get Mom back, we're going to have to make up a story about where she is. I'm thinking we should say she's back in Pasadena, wrapping things up—you know, with the house sale and stuff. How's that sound?"

None of them replied.

To David, coming up with an explanation for Mom's absence felt like turning a page and leaving her behind. He knew Dad was right and they had to do it, but he didn't have to like it.

Dad stopped at the end of the road. In the woods, the house seemed to be waiting for them. It was barely visible in the shadows, with its green paint now weathered to a dull gray. David felt it, though. It was like waking up at night and knowing someone was in the room with you, even when you couldn't see him. You just *knew*.

Dad killed the engine and turned to look at each of them. He said, "Well? Can we keep what happened to Mom a secret?"

Xander looked like he'd been asked to swallow a slug. He nodded.

"Toria?" Dad said.

"For how long?"

"Till we get her back."

"What if they make me tell? What if they torture me?"

Dad thought about it. "If they torture you, you can tell them the truth."

That seemed to satisfy her. "Okay."

Dad smiled at David. He said, "I know *you* can do it, Mr. My-Brother-Punched-Me-in-the-Face."

David said, "If it will help get Mom back."

"It will."

"All right then." He had the feeling that this was an important moment, a decision they would always remember. He hoped it was the start of a successful rescue and not something he would have to talk about in court someday. He squeezed his eyes closed, trying to push from his mind all the courtroom dramas he had seen on TV. There seemed to always be a time when someone made the decision to start lying, and everything went downhill from there. This had better not be that moment for them.

Moving on—because his heart *had* to move on—he said, "What are we gonna do about dinner? I'm starving." He opened the car door and hopped out.

On the way to the house, Xander moved in close to him. "Ever see *Spy Kids*?" he asked.

"You know I have," David said. "We have it on DVD."

"So you know the story. Some kids save their parents from a bad guy who imprisoned them."

David stopped walking. "What's your point?"

Xander shrugged. "The kids weren't always up-front about what they were doing. If they were, someone would have stopped them from rescuing their parents."

David rolled his eyes. "Xander, I hate to break this to you, but that was a movie. This is real life."

Xander chuckled. "What's the difference, Dae?"

CHAPTER

SUNDAY, 7:07 P.M.

While Xander helped Toria start dinner, David and Dad put locks on all the third-floor doors. David kept the screws in the sling with his broken arm, along with a snack-sized bag of Fritos. When Dad needed a screw, David would pull it out and hold it in place. As soon as Dad's power screwdriver drove it into the wall, David released it and watched it shrink shorter and shorter until it was all the way in. They had been working in the third-floor hallway for about a half hour. Six doors were now padlocked shut. Fourteen to go.

At the first door, David had cracked it open and peered in. A fishing rod and thigh-high waders rested on the bench. From the hooks hung a tackle box; a vest with pockets everywhere and fishing flies hooked into a patch of thick, yellow wool where ribbons went on a military shirt; and a floppy, wide-brimmed hat.

David had said, "Fishing stuff."

"Shut the door, David. Let's stay on task." When David hesitated, he added, "These rooms have a way of drawing you in. We've got to be careful."

"Draw you in? Like how?" He popped the last of the Fritos in his mouth.

His father dug around in the shopping bag of hardware. "Haven't you noticed? You kind of *want* to go over?"

David thought about when he had gone into the jungle world. He had threatened to go with or without Xander's help—he wanted to go that bad. And hadn't he decided a little too quickly to go into the World War II village in search of Mom?

"If that's true," he said, "it's scary."

"Like a shark posting signs on the beach saying the water's fine," Dad agreed. He snapped a lock through a ring in the hasp and gave it a couple of quick yanks to make sure it was secure. They moved to the next door.

"What's with these wall lights?" David said.

They stopped in front of one that depicted two warriors in

combat. One was thrusting a spear through the other's chest. The figures stuck out slightly from the surface of the shade, which seemed to be made of stone—a *relief*, his father had called it.

"I don't know," Dad said. His hand reached out toward it but stopped short. He held his fingers inches from the warring figures, as though he was resisting a temptation. "I think they show things from the worlds beyond the doors."

"There's one down there with metal leaves and eyes peering through them," David said. "It could be a tiger."

"And you saw the one with the gladiator?"

David nodded, then something occurred to him. He said, "You know how the items in the antechambers change, and then the worlds beyond change too?"

Dad nodded.

David asked, "So do these wall lamps change?"

Dad raised his eyebrows and looked up the hallway at the lights. "Now that you mention it . . . I don't know. Most of the time I've been here, it's been pretty chaotic. A lot of the lights appear the same until you look closer." He put his hand on David's shoulder and nodded. "Good question."

While he was holding a screw for the next hasp, and Dad was positioning the screwdriver over it, David thought of another one: "What if Mom tries to come back and the door's locked?"

Dad lowered the screwdriver and looked at him for a long moment. "Well . . . my mother never did. I don't think the portals work that way."

"But you don't know."

"No."

David grew quiet.

Finally his dad gripped his arm. "Your mother's a strong woman. I'm sure she's all right."

"She's all right," David repeated, "but she's not *here*."

"She's not here," his father agreed.

It took them another forty-five minutes to put locks on the rest of the doors. When it was done, they stood on the landing and looked down the twisting hallway at their handiwork. The hasps and padlocks attached to every door seemed almost an insult to the old-hotel décor. They were ugly and stark, like a scar on the face of a baby.

His father rattled a fat ring of keys and said, "I'll hold on to these."

"Dad?" David said. "Are the locks supposed to keep us out or keep them in?" He didn't have to say who he meant by "them." They knew about only one person who'd come into their house from another world—the big guy who'd taken Mom—but they all wondered if others could and would.

"Both," Dad answered. "Still hungry? Something smells good."

"We have to eat *Toria's* cooking?" David asked.

"She's always helped in the kitchen." He shrugged. "Guess we'll see how she does."

David nodded, and Dad started down the stairs. As David

was about to follow, he heard something in the hallway softly *clink*—metal on metal. He looked, but didn't see anything. Then his eye caught a lock about halfway up on the left side. It was swinging back and forth.

seventeen

SUNDAY, 8:15 P.M.

As long as David could remember, they had come together as a family for dinner. It didn't matter how scattered they were during the day—Dad at work, Mom on errands, Xander with friends, David playing soccer, Toria at some music lesson or other—dinner reunited them, like bees returning to the hive.

While Mom liked to make it nice, David thought it was Dad who wanted the coming-together in the first place. He called it an "anchor"—keeping them moored together despite their far-flung adventures—and an "island"—a place to see each other and rest from each day's "struggle to stay afloat."

Those were Dad's words on tough days. On better ones, it was something like "a romp in the surf" or "backstroking through the day's travails." When David had asked him what that meant, he had said, "It means staying calm when troubles hit."

After that, David had sometimes found himself actually rotating his arms in a backstroke way to remind himself not to get too freaked-out. Odd thing was, it worked. Pop quizzes, bullies, not doing so well on the field—they lost some of their scariness with a couple pinwheels of his arms. He'd even come to enjoy the puzzled looks the gesture drew.

He raised his right arm now and brought it back and down. He began to lift his left arm, but felt the extra weight on it and the dull pulse of his blood rushing through it, and remembered the cast. He raised it as high as his shoulder, then switched back to his good arm. Sitting next to him, Xander gave him a knowing smile.

Toria had put a place setting in front of their mother's chair. *Sad*, David thought . . . *and a little creepy.*

His sister came in with water glasses, which she set precisely at each plate's one o'clock position. The glass she placed by her mother's plate was the only one that was empty. She gave it a little nod and glanced at the empty chair, as though seeing someone there that David did not. Then she strode back into the kitchen.

Dad, sitting at the head of the table, opposite Mom's place, caught the boys' unease. He said, "It was my idea. In many cultures, families would keep a place at the table for a missing loved one, a son who'd gone off to war or someone who'd . . ." He let the rest of his thought trail off.

David watched him. Dad didn't want to say, "Someone who'd *died*," and David didn't want him to say it.

More quietly, Dad continued, "It reflected that person's place in their hearts. They were gone, but in a way still with them."

Toria came back with a tureen. A ladle rose from steaming yellow liquid. "Chicken noodle soup," she announced.

"You made it yourself?" Xander asked.

"Smells great!" David said, trying to make his enthusiasm sound less forced than Xander's.

She dipped her head. "It's Campbell's." She sat and ladled soup into her bowl, then passed the tureen to Dad. She leaned toward him and whispered. "The *candles*."

"Oh, sorry," Dad said. He stood, patted his pockets, found a lighter. He leaned to light the candle nearest him, then walked around Toria to reach the one on the other side of the table. Between the two candlesticks, Toria had placed an arrangement of flowers and what looked to David like weeds from their yard.

Back in his seat, Dad smiled at each of his children. He held one hand out to Toria and the other to Xander. David was glad to see Xander accept it without hesitation. He and Xander gripped hands as well.

David rested his cast on the table near Mom's place setting. He knew if she were there, she would stretch to grip it. He locked eyes with Toria and could tell she was feeling the same thing he did. Sadness, for sure, but something else: it was somehow more *active* than that, like having a wound poked. It was a stark reminder that Mom *should* have been there, but she wasn't.

Without a word, both David and Toria lifted off their seats to clasp hands across the table. It seemed right to David that it was awkward and uncomfortable. A link in their family chain was missing; they weren't supposed to fit right without it.

After that, they bowed their heads, and Dad prayed. "Dear Heavenly Father, thank You for this food and this family. Please be with our wife and mother. Keep her safe." He was silent for a long time, perhaps searching for words that wouldn't come, or maybe talking privately to God. Finally he said, "Amen," and the kids repeated the word.

"Remember last Sunday?" David asked. "You told Mom we'd go to church this Sunday—'no excuses.'"

Dad frowned. "I wasn't expecting such a doozy of an excuse. But no more. Next week for sure."

David smiled weakly. "That's what Mom said."

"I know. And I mean it. Your mother will kill me if I let things fall apart here."

They ate their soup in silence. Their spoons clinked against the bowls. David didn't intend to slurp his soup, but did anyway. Xander probably intended to and did. David had heard expressions like "the silence was deafening" and someone's "absence filled the room." They had never made sense to him. But now he understood.

"David?" Dad said, startling him out of his thoughts.

David felt something on his cheek and touched it. He had not realized he was that close to crying. *Close?* He *was* crying. He used his napkin to wipe his eyes. "I'm okay."

Toria set down her spoon, walked around the table, and wrapped her arms around him.

Dad found and held his gaze. David had always thought his father resembled the perfect knight. His face was lean and strong, almost muscular; he had a broad forehead, direct eyes, and a slightly cleft chin. David had inherited that cleft, unlike his siblings. He sometimes studied his features in a mirror, wondering from which parent each came and if all of them together made him look strong or weak, like a man or a wuss. His father definitely did not look like a wuss.

As though he had read David's mind, his father said, "It's not unmanly to cry, son." His eyes flicked to Xander, including him, then back to David. "If we didn't have strong feelings, how could we love or fight? When our flesh is cut, we bleed. When our heart is broken, we cry. There's nothing wrong with that. It only becomes a problem when it gets in the way of what you have to do. You can't crumble when others are counting on you."

David sniffed and nodded.

That's what he means, he thought. *He's protecting us. He probably wants to cry himself, even now. But he has a family to protect and a wife to find.*

Dad said, "Do I smell something besides soup, something good?"

"Meat loaf," Toria said with a smile. She released David and ran off to get it.

Dad looked compassionately at his boys. "We'll be okay," he whispered. "You know that, don't you?"

Xander shrugged.

David thought about it, then he smiled and nodded.

"Ta-da!" Toria said. She was wearing oven mitts and carrying a casserole dish. So much steam rose from it, David couldn't make out her features. Then the dish shattered on the floor before he even realized it had slipped from her hands. Toria screamed.

Dad, David, and Xander jumped up from their chairs.

David said, "Did you burn yourself? Are you all right?"

Then all three of them realized she was staring at something. They turned their own gazes toward the door that opened into the foyer.

A man was standing there, smiling.

CHAPTER

eighteen

SUNDAY, 8:41 P.M.

"Hey! Hey!" Dad said. He stepped over the broken casserole dish and ruined meat loaf. As he strode toward the man, Dad's hands came up, as though he intended to physically toss the guy out on his head.

David wanted to shout out a warning. It was the man he had seen in the woods, the one who had watched them fly.

The man raised his palm to Dad, his own warning to keep

Dad at bay. He said, "I'm sorry. I didn't mean to startle you." His voice was deep and smooth.

Despite the urgency his sudden appearance had put into all of them, his words came out slowly. David detected a slight accent he couldn't place.

Dad stopped inches from the man's outstretched hand. He said, "You walk into my *home* and—what?—oops? I don't think so." He stepped closer. His hand touched the man's arm to nudge him toward the door.

"It was unlocked," the man said. "My coming in was . . . habit, I supposed you'd say."

"Habit?"

"You see . . ." The man's voice trailed off. He had scanned the faces of the King children, stopping on David's. His eyes appeared gray and slightly too large for his face, which was lean and muscular. He had thin lips, which seemed to be perfectly horizontal: they offered no hint of a smile or a frown. The man's hairline had ebbed back from his face, giving him a large forehead. His hair, black with threads of silver, was swept back and fell to his shoulders. It looked wiry, like the Brillo pads Mom used to clean their iron skillet.

The man's gaze seemed to reach past David's eyes to examine his thoughts. David fought the urge to run, to get away from his piercing stare, but he couldn't move. The man's eyes held him in place the way a pin holds a bug to a cardboard display.

"Sir!" Dad nearly yelled.

The man pushed his lips into a twisted smile, then snapped his gaze away from David.

He continued talking to Dad, as though he hadn't paused to scare David spitless. "You see, I used to visit this house. I've always found it lovely. Are these your children?"

"What do you mean, 'visit'?" Dad said.

"Your boy," the man said, gesturing toward David. "If I may ask, what happened to his arm?"

"Little accident," Dad answered.

The man nodded knowingly. "Boys will be boys."

"I didn't catch your name," Dad said.

The man's raised palm turned so it became a hand extended in greeting. "Taksidian," he said. "You may call me Jim."

Dad ignored the man's gesture. "Mr. Taksidian, the door is this way. . . ."

Taksidian frowned. "I was hoping we could talk."

"About what?"

"You are Edward King, are you not?"

"You know I am."

"And you own this house?" While he spoke, the man's gaze drifted again to David. Slowly, the man winked at him.

David felt himself on the verge of either passing out or peeing his pants. He mumbled something that he had intended to be "Excuse me," but it didn't come out that way at all. Forcing himself to break away from the man's stare, he walked into the kitchen.

As soon as he knew he was out of sight, he put his back up against the wall and edged close to the doorway. For the second time that day, he found himself eavesdropping on his father's conversation.

"I have to confess to a bout of foolishness," the man said.

"How's that?" his father prodded.

"This house," the man said.

His deep voice reminded David of hypnotists he'd seen in movies. The tone of their voices alone made people want to do what they asked.

"I've admired this house for a long time. I kept telling myself to buy it, but—and here's where I've been foolish—I never thought I needed to hurry. Here you are, proving me wrong."

"Well, Mr. Taksidian, if—"

"Jim, please."

"Jim," Dad said. His voice was softening.

David knew his father would give the man the benefit of the doubt. As though walking into someone else's home could ever be an accident!

Don't cut him any slack, Dad, David thought. *This guy meant to scare us. He knows more than he's letting on.*

Dad went on: "If it's any consolation, this house has been in my family a long time. It was never for sale."

"Really?" the man said. "What about now?"

"I'm sorry?" Dad said.

"I'm willing to make a most generous offer."

David could almost hear the man smiling. He felt something touch his arm, and he jumped.

Toria stood in front of him. She whispered, "What are you doing?"

"Shhh."

She leaned closer. "What's the matter? You don't look so good."

"I'm okay," he said. "Come on." He walked back into the dining room, trying not to look at the man. He stopped at his dad's side and gripped his arm.

"I'm sorry," his dad was saying. "This house is not for sale."

David stared at the man's hand. It was powerful looking, veined and wrinkled. Scars marred the skin, slashing across the knuckles. A thick welt of scar tissue ran up the back of his hand and disappeared into the sleeve of his overcoat. His fingernails were longer than they should have been. *Dracula hands*, he thought.

"Is that something you and Mrs. King have discussed? Perhaps *I* should talk to her. I have a . . . *way* with women."

David felt the muscles in Dad's arm tense up. He tightened his grip. As much as the man deserved it, he thought Dad hitting him was a very bad idea.

nineteen

SUNDAY, 8:52 P.M.

Holding onto Dad's arm as Dad spoke to Mr. Taksidian, David's heart stepped up from a gallop to a headlong run.

Was it his imagination, or had the man's voice taken on a threatening tone when he mentioned Mom? As much as he'd have rather avoided the man's piercing eyes, David looked up to his face.

Dad said, "Your *way* with women has nothing to do with my wife, sir."

The man was looking up toward the second-floor landing, as though expecting to see Mom standing there. He said, "I meant only that she should hear my offer. As I said, it's quite generous."

"She's not here right now."

Dad's voice had taken on a hard edge. David wondered if it was from the stress of having to lie about Mom or because the man's pushiness had made him angry.

"Oh? When will she return? Perhaps I can wait."

Dad said, "She's away. Maybe a couple weeks."

"I see," the man said. His Dracula hand slipped inside his overcoat. It reappeared holding a small pad of paper, which he opened with a flick of a fingernail. His other hand dropped into an outside pocket and produced a pen. He said, "If you'll tell me how to reach her, I'll give her the details directly."

"The house is not for sale," Dad repeated. "Now, if you'll please . . ." He nodded toward the door. "We were just sitting down to dinner."

The man didn't budge. He stood like a statue, casting his awful gaze at Dad's face. David realized that Dad had leaned closer to the man. He was staring him down, not blinking.

Way to go, Dad.

"Houses like this," the man said, "are always more than most people can handle."

When Dad did not respond, the man continued: "You know, not as stable as they look on the surface. A wall might collapse. Other surprises. I would hate . . ." He took the time to look at Xander, then Toria, finally coming to rest on David. "I would *hate* to see anything happen to your lovely family."

"Good night, Mr. Taksidian," Dad said.

The man closed his eyes. He sighed heavily. "Will you at least hear my offer?"

"No."

His eyes opened slowly. He nodded and turned. He opened the front door but did not step through. Without looking back, he said, "Mr. King . . . I have a nasty habit of getting what I want."

Again, Dad said, "Good night, *sir*." The "sir" sounded as sharp as a fist striking a skull.

The man stepped out, and the door closed behind him.

The family didn't move for a long time. They just stared at the door. David wondered if anyone else expected the man to come back through.

Finally Xander went to the door and turned the knob that engaged the dead bolt. He looked at Dad. "What just happened?"

Toria said, "Who *was* that?"

Dad told her, "If you see him again, don't go near him."

"Dad," David said, near a whisper. He was still gripping his father's arm, tighter now. "That was the man I saw in the woods."

"What?" Xander said. "When we were flying? When you fell?"

David looked up at his father and knew right away that Dad had suspected as much.

"But wait," Xander continued. "If he saw David flying or

hovering or whatever it was we were doing, why didn't he say anything about it? I mean, that's gotta be, like, the weirdest thing anyone has ever seen, right? You don't just ignore it."

Toria said, "Maybe he didn't really see David."

"He did," David said, remembering the eyes watching him in the forest. They were the same eyes that had stared him down just now.

Xander stepped closer. "This can't be a coincidence. We move in, Mom gets taken, this guy shows up wanting to buy the place? What's going on?"

Dad didn't answer right away. When he did, his words came slowly. "I don't know who he is or what he wants with this house. But you're right, his showing up isn't a coincidence. He's here because we're here, and he doesn't want us to be. We've got to watch out for him."

"Like we don't have enough going on?" Xander said. "We've gotta find Mom while pretending everything's all right, we gotta watch out for the guy who *took* Mom, and now we have to watch for *this guy*?!"

"What else are we gonna do?" David said.

It was too much for one day. Stepping into some French village during a Nazi attack. The flying—or *whatever* it was they had done in the clearing. Breaking his arm. The doctor's accusation. And now this guy: his sudden appearance, his low measured way of talking, his *eyes*.

David didn't want to let go of his dad. And his other arm

was in a sling. But in his mind he did the backstroke. Just trying to be calm when he had every reason to go crazy.

"I'm not going to pretend this doesn't change things," Dad said. "We'll have to be more careful, we may have to work faster, and we've got to keep our eyes open for dangers coming at us from outside the house."

"Taksidian," Xander said.

Dad nodded. "But in some ways, nothing's changed. We still have to do everything we can to avoid drawing attention to ourselves. Maybe that's more important than ever now."

David said, "Is that your way of saying we still have to go to school tomorrow?"

"No!" Xander said.

Dad smiled. "First day of school. I'm the principal. I think we have to, don't you?"

Xander said, "I say we do nothing but look for Mom. Eat when we have to, sleep when we can. Get Mom, get out of here, and leave this house for Taksidian or whoever else wants it."

Man, that sounded good to David.

But then Dad said, "That would be fine if we knew for sure we could find Mom quickly. My dad spent weeks looking for my mother and never found her."

"That was one person," Xander said. "With all of us working together—"

"And that's why we're going to find her," Dad interrupted. "But I don't think it will be easy . . . or quick."

"If it takes a year, ten years," David said, "I'm in."

"Me too," Toria said.

Xander frowned, but he was nodding. He said, "Okay, we pretend everything is great, and that buys us the time we need to find Mom."

"School tomorrow, then," Dad said. "So let's get to bed early. Toria, how about the two of us rounding up something else for dinner?"

Toria headed down the hall toward the kitchen.

"Xander," Dad said, "would you and David mind cleanup duty?" He nodded his head toward the mess on the floor.

"Awww," David said. "The meat loaf smelled good. We can't have any of it?"

Dad laughed and gave him a push, then went to join Toria in the kitchen.

David touched his arm to stop him. "What about the man? Taksidian?"

Dad squeezed David's shoulder reassuringly. "He's going to do what he's going to do, Dae. Right now all we can do is wait and see what that is."

"He said he was in the house. Do you think he knows about the third floor, the portals?"

Dad thought about it. "There's a reason he wants this place. I imagine it has something to do with this place being special—and what makes it special are the portals."

David bit his lip. "But . . ." He didn't know how to put his feelings into words. It was like having the messiest room in the world: he didn't know where to start to sort it out in his head.

Dad touched his cheek. "Don't worry about it, son. Together, we'll get through whatever we have to. Okay?"

David nodded.

Dad walked down the hall and disappeared into the kitchen.

David stood watching, thinking. *He's going to do what he's going to do.* David didn't like the sound of that.

CHAPTER

SUNDAY, 9:00 P.M.

Mr. James Taksidian—he was used to the name now—stood in front of the house among the trees. Moonlight played against the clapboards, stirred by the shadows of countless leaves. He could still see the oldest boy in the foyer, his back to one of the narrow, leaded windows that flanked the front doors. Absently, he rubbed at the heavy scar on the back of his right hand.

The meeting had not gone as well as he had hoped. A

few more weeks without their wife and mother, a few more encounters with household intruders, and they would have jumped at the opportunity to abandon the house. Ah, but Taksidian was growing older, and less patient. He had fewer years left to do all the things he wanted to do. He didn't have time for pests like the King family.

He had hoped to find more despair and disillusionment. When he started to push them—frightening the boy, implying knowledge of what had happened to the woman—he had witnessed more anger and determination than the fear he had hoped to instill.

One important fact had come from the meeting: he had verified that they were not some random family who had somehow weaseled their way into the house. They belonged. This meant they would not scare so easily. But he had no doubt that he could get them out. If one method did not work, another would. Seeing the resolve in their faces, hearing it in their voices, had convinced him that he had to step up his efforts. The pressure he would apply could crush a . . . He searched for the right metaphor and laughed when he found it. The pressure he would apply could crush a king.

He spun away from the house and headed toward the car he had parked down the road. He laughed again, sure that he knew the outcome of this latest little adventure with the house.

They would run or they would die—he didn't care which.

The last one had fled, and for almost thirty years had left Taksidian alone to do as he pleased. It had been a time of great prosperity.

And he would have his time with the house once again.

CHAPTER

TUESDAY, 11:28 P.M.

Something woke David from a sound sleep. He saw that
Xander was sitting up in bed and thought that his brother had
called to him.

"What?" he said to Xander's dark profile.

"Shhh."

Bam!

David jumped. "Was that a gunshot?" The noise seemed to come from the hallway, but who really knew?

Bam!

"Xander!" David had *felt* the noise that time, coming up through the floor into his bed.

"Daaaaad!" It was Toria. David and Xander threw back their blankets at the same time and hit the floor running.

Bam! Bam!

The vibration shot up into David's feet. Before they reached it, the hallway light turned on. Xander charged through the doorway, with David right behind.

"Daaaaad!"

Bam! Bam! Bam!

Dad was running down the hall toward Toria's room. He reached it ahead of Xander and swung through. Xander and David stopped at the threshold.

Bam! Bam!

David not only felt it in his feet, but also in his arm, which was pressed against the door frame. Toria was sitting up in bed, eyes wide. She reached out and grabbed her father's neck. He lifted her out of bed and scanned the room wildly.

Bam!

Not from this room.

"What is it?" Toria squealed.

Dad said, "I don't know, honey. It's okay." He walked toward the door. David and Xander stepped back into the hall.

Bam!—followed by a crash.

At once, their faces turned toward the ceiling. David touched his father's elbow. "The hallway upstairs."

Dad began walking with Toria in his arms toward the far hallway and the false wall. He stopped in front of his open bedroom door to hand Toria to Xander.

Dad disappeared into his bedroom, then reemerged with the ring of keys he and David had made earlier in the day.

"Stay here," he told them.

"No way!" Xander said. He reached out and grabbed hold of his father's T-shirt.

"Daddy, no!" Toria said.

Bam! Bam! Bam! More crashes. Something *thunked*. The lights in the hall flickered with each sound.

Dad thought about it. He scanned the ceiling.

Bam! Crash!

"Stay behind me," he said. He walked around the corner and stopped.

The false wall was shut tight. The two padlocks they had attached earlier were locked and hanging from their hasps as they had left them.

Bam! Bam!

The lights flickered. The locks swung slightly from the vibration.

Dad strode to the wall. He checked the number on the top lock and started flipping through the keys.

"We should have bought a gun," Xander said. He stooped to set Toria down on her feet. "Why didn't we buy a gun?"

Dad got the first lock off and squatted in front of the lower one.

The bat Dad and Xander had used against the big man who had taken Mom had been destroyed when one of the portal doors shut on it. Not that it had done any good, David thought. Still, he would have felt better if one of them carried something, anything more than keys.

The boxes that had been piled up against the wall and then scattered when the man had come for Mom were still there. Some were turned over, none of them neatly arranged. It looked as though the boxes themselves had been running from the sounds and stopped when the humans arrived. David looked in one and found only clothes. Another contained books. Not quite sure what he was looking for.

From the third box he pulled a toy rifle. He hadn't played with it for at least a year, but he hadn't wanted to toss it out, either. The stock and forward grip were made of wood, the barrel of steel. At one time it had been a cap gun, but that part of it hadn't worked for a long time. David held it by the barrel, feeling its heft. He caught Xander looking at him, and David nodded: *Yeah, this'll clock somebody good.*

Dad had the false wall open and was stepping through to the next door. David hurried through the opening and over the next threshold to follow his father up the stairs.

Dad was tiptoeing now, so David did too. He had forgotten Xander and Toria were behind him until he heard the creak of a step and his brother's breathing close behind.

Bam!

Toria let out a yip.

David jumped. He almost lost his balance and fell backward down the stairs. Xander's hand pressed into his back and righted him.

The noise had been earsplitting. Definitely a gunshot.

Their father was crouched low at the top of the stairs, not quite on the landing. He was trying to peer around the corner and down the long, jagged hallway.

"What is it?" David whispered.

"Can't see. Too dark." Dad edged up onto the landing, gesturing for them to stay back. He moved toward the hallway on his hands and knees, stopping when his head was just below the light switch. He stayed like that a long time, perhaps listening or hoping his eyes would adjust to the dark.

David expected another gunshot at any moment. For some reason, he didn't think Dad would be hit, but he would jump back to get out of the way and crash into the three of them. The whole family would tumble down the stairs and land in a heap at the bottom. The flight did not have a handrail, so he crouched low and gripped the edge of the landing. Xander crowded up behind him.

In the murky light of the staircase's single dim bulb, David saw his father's hand finally rise to the switch. The hallway lit up in that strange way that was becoming familiar to David: it was somehow different from other light, seeming to flicker like fire, without actually flickering at all.

Dad made a noise David didn't understand, kind of a surprised moan.

"Dad?" he whispered. When his father didn't answer, David reached out and touched his foot.

Dad startled and swung his head around to look back. David didn't like what was in his eyes.

"What is it?" David whispered.

Dad shook his head. Slowly he stood, staying close to the wall.

Can't be some madman with a gun, David figured, *but what would scare Dad without chasing him away?*

He rose and stepped onto the landing behind his father. He looked past him and gasped.

Every lock and hasp they had installed that day was lying on the floor. They were closest to the wall opposite the doors they had secured, as though ripped from the doors and frames with great force.

He heard the others coming up behind him. He stepped around Dad for a better look. Across from the first door the wainscoting was damaged. Farther up, opposite the second door, one of the wall fixtures had broken. A large piece of it—featuring the prancing legs of a horse—lay on the floor.

Sawdust, splinters, even pencil-sized strips of wood fanned out from each door.

"The locks just blew off," Xander said behind him. "Look. They hit the walls hard enough to break the wood. That light fixture is higher than the lock was. The lock must have come off with so much force it actually *flew*."

"Did someone kick the doors open, you think?" David asked. He looked back at his dad.

Dad's eyes roamed the hall, taking in the locks and splintered wood. He whispered, "The doors don't open into the hall. They couldn't have been kicked open."

Toria spoke up, her voice shrill. "Is somebody here? Are there people behind the doors?"

That creeped David out. He felt his stomach tighten. His eyes darted from door to door, as far as the crooked hallway would let him. He caught a glimpse of something. He said, "Dad? About halfway up on the right—one of the doors still has a lock."

"Not only that," Xander said. "It's moving."

CHAPTER

twenty-two

Xander was right. The lock was vibrating. It seemed to move faster and faster. Then the sound of it rattling against the hasp reached them: *click-click-click-click-click-click* . . .

Xander said, "What does that mean?"

Dad just shook his head.

David pressed up close to him and stayed there as they moved closer to the door. He felt Xander's hand on his shoulder. David was doing the same thing with Dad: it was a way of staying close without having to pay attention: all of their focus was on that door.

As they drew nearer, Dad lifted the keys.

"*Don't*," David said.

"Let's go downstairs," Toria agreed.

Dad hesitated. "Look, guys," he said. "Maybe there's a reason this door and only this door still has a lock on it."

David's head began to hurt. He squeezed his eyes shut and said, "Just do it."

Keys rattled, and he opened one eye to see this father select a key and let all the others drop away from it to settle at the bottom of the ring. Dad took a step closer. David went with him. Xander kept his hand on David's shoulder.

The vibrating of the lock became faster: *clickclickclickclickclickclick.*

Toria said, "Is there something on the other side of the door doing that?"

Dad pressed his palm to door. He said, "I don't think so. I don't feel it coming through the door."

David was between his father and the door. He leaned his shoulder to the door and felt nothing.

Dad reached out with the key. David saw that Dad's hand was shaking, almost as quickly as the lock. David heard the key tap against the lock as Dad tried to find the—

Bam!

The lock and hasp flew away from the door—so fast David

saw only a blur marking its trajectory. It struck Dad's hand. He yelled and pulled his arm back.

"Go!" he yelled. "Back! Back!" He swung his arms out and reversed, forcing David, Xander, and Toria to move back toward the landing as well. His hand grazed David's cheek.

David felt warm wetness and wiped at it. His fingers came away bloody. As they continued moving away from the door, he focused on Dad's hand, held out to corral his children: blood poured from a gash along the back of his hand. David could see that the skin around it had already turned dark—black-and-blue, people called it, but this was mostly black.

"Dad—" David said. "Your hand!"

"Go, David! Go!"

At the landing, they stopped.

Dad continued holding his arms out like a guard keeping back a crowd. David stared at the wound. It was leaking like a broken bottle of ketchup. But it wasn't ketchup, and David's stomach turned.

"What happened?" Xander said.

"It just flew off," Dad said.

Toria said, "It hurt my ears."

"Your scream hurt mine," Xander said.

"That was David," she said.

Dad hushed them. They stood quietly in the hall, watching the door, listening.

Finally Xander whispered, "If that lock had hit somebody, they'd be dead."

"Xander," David said, "it did." He turned his eyes back to Dad's hand.

"Dad!" Xander said.

Toria made an "Oohhh" sound.

"I'm all right," Dad said.

Xander said, "That doesn't look all right."

Dad inspected his hand and tucked it close to his chest. "It looks worse than it is." He glared down the hall. "Are there any more locks?"

"Daddy," Toria said, "can't we check tomorrow? Your hand . . ."

David saw the struggle in Dad's face. He wanted to know what was going on. He wanted to know *now*.

After a moment, Dad said, "Okay, we'll see what's up tomorrow. After school."

"We still have to go?" Xander said.

"We've already been through this, Xander," Dad said.

Dad stayed on the landing until David, Xander, and Toria were at the bottom of the stairs. He took a last look into the hallway, flipped off the lights, and came down. His hand had soaked his T-shirt, making it look to David like he was holding together a hideous wound in his abdomen.

twenty-three

Monday, 12:01 a.m.

Together they washed and dressed Dad's hand in the master bathroom. When Dad stuck his hand under the faucet, David wanted to turn away. He expected torn muscles, veins, and bones. But Dad had been right. It wasn't as awful as it had looked. A deep, long gash, lots of bruising.

David and Xander were almost back to their bedroom when their father called to them. Dad was on the other end of the second-floor hallway, in front of his own bedroom. Toria stood with him, holding his hand.

"What?" Xander said.

"Let's stay together tonight," Dad said.

"*Sleep* together?"

"Sounds good to me," David said.

Dad said, "We'll make beds for you in here." He gestured toward his bedroom. "Come on, Xander."

Xander shook his head. "Hold on."

The boys went into their bedroom to gather their pillows and blankets.

"This is nuts," Xander grumbled.

"Why?" David said. "You know what they say: safety in numbers."

Xander scowled at him and stormed out of the room. David hurried to catch up, and the two of them, laden with bedding, marched down to the master bedroom.

Toria was already under the covers in the big bed. David dropped his pillow and blankets beside the bed, on Dad's side. Xander kept hold of his stuff, as though setting it down would mean he was cool with their all staying together, which he obviously wasn't. Dad pushed a bit of blanket under Toria and came around to help David set up his sleeping area.

"How long are we going to have to sleep in the same room?" Xander asked.

"We've got to watch out for each other," Dad said.

"Can't you and Toria stay in here, and David and I sleep in our own room?"

Dad positioned David's pillow, sat on the floor beside it, and crossed his legs. He sighed. "It's better this way, Xander."

"How is it better?"

Dad said, "Safety in numbers."

Xander rolled his eyes. "Yeah, I heard. So what, are we going to stay together *all* the time?"

"As much as possible," Dad said. "At least at night."

"So who's gonna go to the bathroom with me?"

"Xander," Dad warned.

"No, really." Xander dropped his bedding on the floor. "We're going to be like prisoners!"

"Shhh," Toria said and rolled over. She flipped her pillow, covering her head with it.

Dad closed his eyes, opened them again. "I was thinking more like the buddy system."

"Okay," Xander said. "The buddy system means two people together, right, Dae? Isn't that what they told you in your scuba classes?"

"Yeah," David said quietly. He didn't want to get in the middle of this argument.

Dad just looked at him.

"See?" Xander continued. "Two people. David and me. You and Toria."

Dad leaned back, propping himself up with his undamaged

hand. He rolled his head in a complete circle. He looked as tired as David felt.

"I don't know, Xander. The guy who took Mom. This new person, Taksidian. The locks not helping one *bit!*"

David could tell it was all getting to him. He wanted to tell Xander that they should just do what Dad said. Give the man a break. But Xander was as stressed as Dad was. And he did have a point. In the end, David bit his tongue and busied himself with ensuring his makeshift bed was laid out just right.

"Dad," Xander said, "I just don't think it's practical. You said that thing about safety in numbers, but there's also something about getting more done in teams, isn't there? When we're here, when we're not out pretending everything's okay, we have a lot to do."

Dad groaned and got to his feet. He put his hands at the small of his back and bent backward. "All right," he said. "If I had my way, we'd lash ourselves to each other and never be separated again." He stepped closer to Xander. "I can't stand the thought of something happening to one of you. Overprotective, I guess."

Xander shrugged. "I suppose you have good reason to be."

"Stay in here tonight," Dad said. "Humor me. Tomorrow, you and David can go back to your own room." He waggled a finger at Xander. "But you're buddies, you hear? You stay together."

Xander smiled. "Gotcha."

"David, you hear?" Dad said.

"Stick with Xander," David confirmed. Then he watched with relief as Xander wrapped his arms around their father and hugged him.

CHAPTER

twenty-four

MONDAY, 12:40 A.M.

David came out of sleep slowly. Like rising from deep under water to the surface. It was rough seas, and the waves jostled him back and forth. Then he realized it was Xander, shaking him gently. In the glow of a night-light, he could see Xander smile.

"What do you want?" he grumbled. "I'm tired."

"But, Dae, I have to go to the bathroom. Don't you want to come?"

"No, go yourself."

Dad had not really meant buddying up for bathroom trips, and Xander knew it. Even if Dad had meant for them to stay together for everything, even this, Xander would not have obeyed. He was just trying to get back at David for not supporting him in front of Dad.

Or something . . . like that . . .

David was going back under, into that dark deep, leaving the surface way behind.

Then up again he went, waking once more under Xander's shaking hand.

"Xander! I said *no*. Go yourself."

"I did," Xander said. "I saw something! You gotta come look." He was whispering, but his tone was excited, maybe even scared.

David rose up on an elbow. "What is it?"

Xander touched his lips with a finger. "Shhh."

They both looked at Dad's sleeping form on the bed. Heavy, rhythmic breathing said he was fast asleep. Xander jerked his head toward the bedroom door, rose, and crept toward it. David followed. When they were in the hallway, Xander leaned back in to pull the door closed.

"Now what?" David said.

"Come here." Xander walked down the hall, then began to descend the staircase.

"Xander, wait!"

"It's out front," he said.

"What were you doing out front?"

"I just looked out the window. I thought I heard something." He went the rest of the way down and peered through a window next to the door. "Yeah," he said. "Look."

He moved away.

David touched his nose to the glass. Beyond the porch, the mist swirled lazily over the forest floor, glowing slightly in the moonlight. The trunks of the trees, their branches and leaves were blacker than the shadows they cast. They made David imagine that the house was in the palm of some giant hand, and the trees were fingers.

"Xander, I don't see any—"

But then he did: there was a man out there. He was standing halfway to the dirt road, the trees rising all around him. The mist glowed behind him, making his silhouette stand out.

"He was in that exact spot when I first saw him," Xander said. "I don't think he's moved at all."

David could not take his eyes off the figure. "Maybe he's dead."

Xander stepped to the window on the other side of the door. "Dead? Standing up?"

Just then, the figure did move. One shoulder seemed to come up as the other went down, as though the person had shifted his weight from one foot to the other. Both Xander and David pulled in a sharp breath.

"Do you think it's Taksidian?" David wondered out loud.

"I bet."

"Why? What does he think he'll see?"

"Maybe he's waiting for us to leave so he can do something to the house," Xander suggested. "Or he's just trying to freak us out."

"It's working," David said.

"This place is so weird, maybe it attracts weird people."

David thought about that. He said, "It attracted us."

Xander said nothing. The boys watched the watcher for a couple minutes. In that time, he appeared to shift or sway twice.

David said, "Do you think he can see us?"

Xander looked back around them, at the dark foyer and the upstairs landing. "Not unless he has cat eyes."

"Should we tell Dad?"

"Let him sleep. What's he going to do?"

"Chase the guy away," David said. "Call the cops."

"They won't do anything."

"He's on our property," David said.

"So they make him back up thirty feet. Would that make you happy?"

David imagined the guy thirty feet farther away, but still out there, still watching. He said, "I guess not." He turned away from the window to look at Xander. "So what do we do?"

"Go back to bed."

"What if he's there in the morning?"

"We'll make him an omelet," Xander said.

"I mean it."

Xander pushed away from the glass, shrugged, and headed up the stairs. "Dad will be up then. He'll figure out something."

That wasn't the answer David wanted. He looked back through the window. The mist appeared to be crawling up the figure's legs, like snakes or flames. David felt a chill streak up his spine. Getting to sleep again wasn't going to be easy.

He turned away and started up the stairs, thinking he could still feel the man watching.

CHAPTER

twenty-five

MONDAY, 6:40 A.M.

David couldn't even think of the word that described the
nightmare he was about to face: new school, new kids, new
teachers, new town . . . his mom had just been kidnapped . . .
and they were supposed to act like everything was normal.
Just another day on planet Earth. Isn't the weather lovely
today?

Dad and Toria whipped up a breakfast of French toast

and sausage. They took their sister to her elementary school, and Dad went in to meet the teacher. Xander sat in the front passenger seat, looking tired and glum.

"You all right?" David asked.

"What do you think?" he answered.

They arrived at Pinedale Middle and Senior High a half hour early. Dad wanted to greet the parents as they dropped off their kids. His hand was bandaged, the yellow of ointment, the red of blood barely showing through. He joked about telling the parents he'd hurt his hand disciplining one of his kids. "But nowadays," he said, "we'd better not go there."

David frowned. "Especially after what the doctor said."

Dad looked at his hand, one side, then the other. "If anyone asks, I'll tell them I hurt it fixing up the house. How about you boys join me in saying hi to everyone?"

"Like some kind of don't-we-make-a-cute-family thing?" Xander said. "I don't think so."

"Great way to meet your classmates."

"Dad." Xander rolled his eyes.

"David?" Dad looked at him hopefully.

"I'm with Xander," David said. "I don't wanna get beat up my first day."

"Go, then, go," Dad said, waving them away.

Without saying another word, the brothers walked through the front doors and turned right. There was a sign on a portable stand telling them they were heading toward the grade 6–8 classrooms. Through the windows that lined the wall on their right, they could see Dad standing on the curb, waiting for cars and students. On their left were lockers and classrooms. At the end of the hall, they could go through double doors into the cafeteria or turn left into another hallway. They turned and approached locker number 119. It didn't look like anything special.

Say that after portaling to and from the linen closet, David thought.

Neither of them could believe they hadn't told Dad about it. Between Mom's abduction and trying to deal with it, the linen closet had slipped their minds.

Xander said, "Maybe subconsciously we don't *want* to tell him."

"Doesn't he already know?"

"He's never said anything."

David nudged Xander. "Want another sausage link?"

Xander gave him a puzzled look, then smiled. He eyed the locker. "I don't know . . ."

"There and back, no big deal."

Xander glanced toward the main hallway and its wall of big windows. "Uhh . . ." he started.

David followed his gaze. Across the grassy courtyard, beyond the picnic benches and flagpole, was the student drop-off point. Dad was standing at the curb, grinning right at them. He raised his bandaged hand and waved.

The boys waved back. David said, "I guess maybe later, huh?"

••••••••

When he got there, David's homeroom was empty. A brown lunch bag sat on the teacher's desk, next to a stack of papers and spiral notebooks, so he guessed she'd been there and gone off somewhere. Mrs. Moreau, according to the class schedule Dad had brought home. He unslung his backpack and leaned it against the side of the desk. In Pasadena, backpacks were banned from classrooms, but Dad had said they were still okay here—just more evidence that Pinedale hadn't caught up with the rest of the world.

The windows at the back of the classroom looked out onto an athletic field. Three older boys were on the track that circled a large grassy area. Two were jogging; the other was either in the middle of some extreme stretching exercise or was hoping to replace a contortionist next time the circus came through town. The room was smaller than the ones David was used to. He counted the desks: four rows of five desks each. In Pasadena, only private schools limited their class size to twenty. He supposed Pinedale was too puny to have big classrooms.

He walked around the teacher's desk to a bulletin board on the far wall. There were notices about the hot-lunch program; chess and computer club meetings; a list of fund-raisers—entertainment books, popcorn sales, cake walk: it was enough to make David wonder if they were supposed to be students or salespeople. Sports announcements—once again, it grated on him that the school didn't sponsor an seventh-grade soccer team. Supply lists. Emergency exit procedures. Where to park. How to drive. When to eat. If David had to read all this, if he had to *know* it, he would go out of his mind.

Walking past the teacher's desk again, something caught his eye: his father's name on a piece of paper. Not unusual, given his position at the school. But this wasn't a memo from him or about him. Someone had handwritten his name—Edward King—in the margin of a newspaper. Next to it was a drawing of a face with mean eyes under a V-shaped brow. Horns poked through the hair, and the mouth was full of fangs. A balloon speech box started at his mouth and disappeared under a stack of papers.

He reached to move the stack away so he could read the words. Before his fingers touched the stack, a voice startled him.

"You must be David."

He spun to see a woman pressing a sheath of papers to her chest with both hands, glaring at him. She was in her forties and birdlike—not in the dainty way, but angular and severe. She was thin and tall and slightly stooped, reminding David of a vulture. Adding to the image was the fuzzy gray sweater draped over her shoulders. The dress underneath was bright red.

Her frown disappeared so quickly, David wasn't positive he had seen it at all. In fact, her whole countenance seemed to change in a heartbeat from cruel to kind, but maybe it had been a trick of the light. He wasn't sure her grin was any better than the scowl he thought he'd first seen. It reminded him of a

T-shirt Xander had once owned: a wicked, beady-eyed troll rubbing his scaly-clawed hands together. The slogan under it read *Trust me.*

"Yes, ma'am," he said, thinking he sounded pretty together. Her eyes flicked to the desktop, compelling him to add: "I was just . . . um . . ."

Think!

" . . . looking for information about . . . the chess club."

Her eyebrows went up. They were bushy things more suited to Russian presidents. "Oh, do you play?"

"I try."

"What's your favorite opening move?"

"Pawn . . . to . . ." He felt himself smile. "I'm just starting, really."

"Well," she said, striding toward him. He took a step back. She set the sheath of papers down, covering the cartoon figure of his father. "Mr. Campbell runs the chess club. He'd love to have you. I can introduce you, if you'd like."

"I'll find him when I have more time, thank you."

She held out a long, bony talon. "I'm Mrs. Moreau. Nice to meet you."

David didn't think the hesitation he felt showed as he reached for her hand. It was cold, and he could feel the bones through paper-thin flesh. "David King, ma'am."

He went to withdraw his hand, but she wouldn't give it back. Instead, she put her other hand over his as well.

She said, "I met your father. Such a nice man. How are you liking our little slice of heaven?"

All kinds of images went through David's mind. First, he thought of the piece of Boston Cream pie at the diner last week. Hadn't the waitress called *it* a slice of heaven? Then he guessed she was talking about the school, but who in their right mind would use the word *heaven* to describe a school?

His confusion must have shown, for she added, "Pinedale. Don't you just love it?"

David brightened. "Ah, yes. It's . . ."

Far from Pasadena. Isolated. Smaller than the mall I'm used to. Creepy.

" . . . lovely!"

She leaned toward him, as if sizing up the meal he'd make. She said, "I can't wait to meet Mrs. King."

David opened his mouth and shut it again. "Uh . . . that would be nice," he said lamely.

She released her grip on his hand, and he pulled it back quickly.

She said, "Whatever happened to your arm?"

"Fell out of a tree."

She aimed her beady eyes at his arm for a long time, as if reading the truth from it. She pressed her lips together and nodded. Her not saying anything was worse than questioning him about his fall or even flat-out calling him a liar. He felt the urge to blurt out what had really happened . . . and along with it all the weirdness he'd seen since coming to her little slice of heaven . . . and what had happened to Mom too.

You wanna meet Mrs. King? he thought. *Pack your bags, lady, cause it's a long trip.*

She laughed, snapping him out of his . . . what was that? *Freak-out time* sounded about right.

"You have that deer-in-the-headlights look," she said. "I don't blame you. New town, new school, and you go and hurt yourself." She fixed her eyes on him. Slowly she said, "And I hear you're moving into the old Konig place."

CHAPTER

MONDAY, 8:22 A.M.

"Ma'am?" David said.

"Your house, the Victorian outside of town?"

David nodded. He thought, *Let's not talk about the house, okay?*

She smiled and moved her attention to the papers on her desk. "Lot of work, old house like that. But once it's fixed up, it'll be lovely."

Words and laughter, the squeak of sneakers on tile, drew

their attention to the classroom entrance. Three boys were barreling in, pushing each other, breaking their conversation off when they saw Mrs. Moreau and David.

"Boys!" she said. "How was your summer?"

They nodded, mumbled, "Good" and "Okay."

"Ben, Marcus, Anthony—this is David. He's just moved here from . . ." She swung her gaze back to David. "L.A.?"

"Pasadena."

The boys gave him "hi's" and nods, and he returned them.

One of the kids—David thought his name was Anthony—whose broad shoulders and solid chest would make him prime linebacker material in a few years—said, "What happened to you?"

David raised his elbow in the sling. "Just fell out of a tree." Each time he said it, the half-truth got easier. Maybe he'd believe it someday as well.

"And that shiner," one of the other boys said. "The tree beat you up too?"

That got them all laughing.

"Uh," David said. He touched the bruise around his eye. It was still tender. "I . . . my brother punched me."

"Why?" Another of the boys asked. This one was Ben, if Mrs. Moreau had said their names in the order they stood. He wore glasses and looked like the sort of kid who said "why" a lot.

David shrugged. "Just playing around."

"Is he bigger than you?" Anthony asked. They moved closer, totally ignoring the teacher now.

"He's fifteen."

Ben said, "Does he beat you up a lot?"

The boy who hadn't yet spoken, Marcus, said, "I have a big sister who beats me up all the time."

Anthony pushed him. "She's a girl, dude! You baby!"

The tallest of the three, Marcus didn't look like a baby. He looked big enough to give Xander a hard time. David wondered what kind of monster his sister must be.

More kids streamed in—a guy and four or five girls.

Mrs. Moreau clapped her hands and said, "Everyone find a desk. Anywhere's fine for now. Mr. King, it would do me a great honor if you would sit up here by me." She gestured toward a desk that was front and center. The other kids laughed and stumbled over each other getting to the back of the room.

"Yes, ma'am," David said. He wasn't sure whether he wanted his disappointment to show or not. He didn't want to get on her bad side, but if she knew he wasn't happy there, she might let him move. He retrieved his backpack and took his seat.

Mrs. Moreau sat behind her desk and began squaring the piles of papers. For a few moments she seemed intent on her work, not much interested in the students filling her classroom. Without looking up she tugged the newspaper with his father's caricature on it out from under the stacks of paper, folded it, and dropped it into a desk drawer. Only then did her eyes venture beyond her desk.

"Ladies. Nice to see you," she said. Then, looking beyond David, "Gentlemen, welcome back."

David glanced around shyly, nodding when he caught someone's eye. Several girls had their heads together, glancing at him and giggling. He turned back to find Mrs. Moreau watching him from the corner of her eye. He looked away quickly, not sure if he should acknowledge her attention or pretend he hadn't noticed.

Before he realized it, the classroom had filled up. A bell sounded to mark the beginning of the period, and a few students, who had been standing, rushed to their desks.

Six hundred miles from the last school he had attended, but still so many things were the same: the glare of the fluorescents competing with the daylight; the little noises of chair legs scraping on the floor, cleared throats, the tick of the clock; the mingling odors of a dozen different shampoos and laundry detergents, sweat. David heard the murmur of persistent whispering and wondered if they were whispering about him.

The teacher used her palm as a gavel against a stack of handouts. "Quiet down," she said. "We have a lot to go over and a lot of papers to distribute, some for you and some to take home to your parents. Let's start with roll call." She began with "Abernathy, Jennifer" and proceeded down an alphabetical list, last name first.

David tried to pay attention, tried to remember each name,

though he wasn't turning to see which student it belonged to. Another reason sitting up front stunk.

Mrs. Moreau called "Jennings, Anthony." David thought the guy responding "here" sounded like the Anthony he had met.

"King, David."

"Here," David said.

The room around him erupted in quiet laughter and whispered comments: "King David? Ohhh."

"Did you kill Goliath?"

"Isn't that the naked statue?"

The last one brought a new burst of giggles from the girls and a few *harr-harrs* from the boys.

David felt the eyes of his classmates on the back of his head like raindrops blowing into him. He almost cringed, tucking his head down into his shoulders, but stopped himself.

Just wait it out, he thought. *Don't say anything. You'll just give them more to laugh about.* He was only glad his name wasn't Arthur.

"Hey! Hey!" Mrs. Moreau snapped. Her palm had become a gavel once more. "We do *not* poke fun at people's names. David's name has a rich and regal legacy. When the David you're thinking of was just a boy, he killed a lion with his bare hands."

Several "oohs" around him.

Shhh, he thought, *you're making it worse.*

But she continued: "And he was probably no older than any of you, than *our* David himself, when he slew the giant Goliath with a single stone."

Several kids went, "Ooohhhh!"

Someone asked, "Was he *naked* when he *sleeeeew* him?"

The entire class cracked up.

David felt his face flush. No doubt his face was as red as Mrs. Moreau's dress. His head got heavier, and it was harder not to let it sink between his shoulders.

Mrs. Moreau's hand slammed down with a *bang!* She stood up from her chair and said, "Clayton!"

Don't do it . . . don't do it . . .

She did it. "You can take that smart mouth to the office right now."

David let his head drop. She had just made sure that Clayton's comment about nakedness and "slewing" giants would be passed on to every student in the school, and David would be reminded about it the whole year.

"What?" Clayton protested.

"You heard me, young man."

From the heavy sigh and banging, David knew Clayton was obeying, but was not happy about it. From the corner of David's eye, Clayton came into view. He was a stocky kid, brown hair, freckles. He wasn't mean-looking, just a twelve-year-old kid. When he was almost to the door, Mrs. Moreau stopped him.

"And Clayton?" she said, almost sweetly. "Do you know whom to ask for?"

Oh no! David felt his eyelids stretching until he thought his eyeballs would fall out onto the desk. He shook his head *no* at Mrs. Moreau, but her attention was on Clayton.

Clayton glared at her, his lips tight.

Her thin lips pursed before opening them to squawk, "Ask for *Mr.* King, our new principal."

Clayton's eyes grew as wide as David's and snapped over to him. Shocked whispers filled the air like buzzing bees.

"Yes, Clayton," Mrs. Moreau continued, "David's father. You may call him King Edward if you're still feeling smart when you get there."

Clayton frowned, shook his head, and pushed out of the door.

David was certain his face would remain red forever.

Mrs. Moreau took her seat again. She cleared her throat, checked a sheet of paper in front of her, and said, "Krakauer, Amy."

CHAPTER

twenty-seven

Monday, 4:10 p.m.

"And after that, everyone kept calling me King David!"

In the front seats of the 4Runner, Dad and Xander nodded knowingly.

"It's embarrassing," David said. He made a face at Toria, who was sitting in the backseat with him.

She tilted her head and stuck out her bottom lip, feeling for him.

"Get used to it," Dad said.

Xander twisted around in his seat. "Nobody's said that to you before, back in Pasadena?"

David shrugged. "Sometimes, but it wasn't mean. These guys are mean."

"Mean how?"

"You know, little-kid-giant-killer and . . ." His voice trailed off.

"What?"

"The . . . Michelangelo thing."

Xander laughed. "You're too sensitive, Dae."

"It's embarrassing," he repeated.

"What Michelangelo thing?" Toria asked.

Xander said, "It's a statue—"

"Nothing!" David said. "Can we drop it already?"

Xander grinned. "You're just—"

"Okay, that's enough," Dad said. He slapped Xander's thigh. He moved the inside rearview mirror to find David's face. "Otherwise, how was it, Dae?"

"All right, I guess."

"I'm Star of the Week in October," Toria said brightly.

"Your birthday week?" Dad asked. He moved the mirror off of David to find her.

"No . . . some other kid has a birthday that week too. They gave it to him."

"That's not fair," Xander declared. "You're a girl; you should've got it."

"Tell that to Mrs. Varley," Toria said. "She doesn't believe in girls first or any of that. She even said there's no difference, so there should be no special treatment."

Dad braked at a crosswalk. He signaled for a couple of kids to cross. To Toria he said, "Do you believe there's no difference?"

"Well, of course there is!" She could have added: *Duh.*

"I mean beyond the obvious," Dad said. "Should boys treat girls special?"

"We *are* special."

"And boys aren't?" David asked.

Toria stuck her nose in the air. "Mom says boys would be like rocks if it weren't for girls."

"*Rocks?*" David said.

"God made girls special, so we can teach boys how to feel."

David shook his head. "I don't need girls to teach me how to feel."

"Guys fight and girls *looove.*" Toria strung out the last word in a swooning, romantic way and batted her eyes.

"I *know* Mom didn't say *that,*" Xander said.

"I said that," Toria said.

David liked talking about Mom. It kept her with them, in a way. He said, "I wonder what she would have put in our notes today."

Toria beamed. "Oh, yeah! Mom always put notes in our lunches on the first day of school."

Xander crinkled his nose. "Mushy, corny ones. Half the note

was *I love you this* and *I'm proud of you that*. The other half never made sense."

David grinned. "Like last year. She told me not to rip my pants or try to open doors with my face." He shook his head. "What was that about?"

"She told me not to put Skittles in my nose," Toria said.

Xander said, "And she never even *tried* to explain them. She'd just look at you like *Whatta ya mean, you don't get it?*"

They all laughed. That was Mom. She wasn't very good at *telling* jokes. She either forgot the punchline or said it too soon or set it up all wrong. But her lunch-box notes had always made David smile, and they'd all laugh about them later.

"You know," Dad said, "she gave me notes too."

Xander looked surprised. "She did?"

Dad tilted his head. "Once, a long time ago—Xander, you were just a baby, David and Toria, you weren't born yet—she sent me off to my first day on a teaching job with a brown-bag lunch. I put it in the refrigerator in the faculty break room. There were half a dozen brown bags just like it, and one of the other teachers got mine by mistake. He found the note, and it said, 'Honey, don't forget to glue on your hair.' I had a big ol' mop of hair back then, but from that day on, I could never convince anyone that it was really mine. I would pull on it and invite them to yank on it, too, but they would just laugh and say I must use good glue."

They all laughed. Xander lifted his own hair on both sides to show both its volume and authenticity.

"Let me tell you," Dad said, "for a guy with lots of hair, that was devastating."

Toria pulled at her hair with both hands; David did the same with his one good hand. Together they said, "I must have used the good glue!"

Dad remembered more. "At the faculty Christmas party, I tried to get her to admit she was joking, but she played it straight. She never actually said I was bald, but she said things like, 'There's nothing wrong with male-pattern baldness. Look at Sean Connery.' As sweet and innocent as can be."

"Is that when you started calling her Gee instead of Gertrude?" Xander asked.

David added the line he'd heard his dad say so many times: "Because she definitely isn't a *Gertrude!*"

"Nah," Dad said. "She'd been going by Gee since she was a little girl. She was named after her grandmother, but her parents knew right away that she wasn't going to live up to the old-fashioned prim and properness that name brings to mind."

"What do you think she should have been named?" Toria said.

Dad smiled. "Honey."

As the SUV progressed up Main Street toward home, their laughter faded. David knew that the others were thinking of Mom, just as he was.

After a minute Xander said, "What are we going to do? About getting her back?"

"I was thinking," Dad said. "We're going to need a central place to figure out that house, to gather everything we know and everything we learn about those rooms upstairs."

"A war room," Xander said.

"A mission control center, like NASA's," David suggested.

Dad nodded. "You've got the right idea." He pulled off the main drag into a drive-in diner. It was the kind of place where you ordered from your car and they hooked your tray of food onto the car window. He smiled at them and raised his eyebrows. "Who's up for an ice cream?"

CHAPTER

twenty-eight

MONDAY, 5:18 P.M.

"Okay, where?" David asked.

The whole family was in the library. Boxes from their old house were stacked there, waiting to be unpacked—the movers had come on Friday, and Mom had been kidnapped Sunday night: almost everything they owned was still boxed up and would probably stay that way for a while. Dad had identified the cartons that would be most useful to their task, the ones from his home office.

David had spotted a dry-marker board and pulled it out from between a wall of boxes and the built-in library shelves. Now he needed to know where to take it: what part of the house would become their mission control center?

"How about this room?" Xander said. "It's got shelves. It's close to the kitchen."

"Nah," David said. "If we have to go back and forth between the control room and the portals, this is too far away. Two flights of stairs and the other end of the house."

Dad said, "Besides, it's open to the foyer. Anybody coming over would see it. We don't want that."

"What about in the hallway on the third floor?" Toria chimed, apparently stunned by her own brilliance. "Right there next to the doors and everything!"

"That's a little *too* close for me," David said. "The way those locks came off, and everything that's happened up there . . ."

"It'd be like having a war room right on the front lines," Xander agreed. "Bullets zinging around—you'd never get any planning done."

"How about the servants quarters'?" Dad said. "Big room. Has its own bathroom. Right at the base of the stairs leading up to the portals."

"Perfect," Xander said.

"I like it," David agreed. He walked out of the room with the dry-marker board, heading for the stairs.

Xander lifted a box that had the word *Mac* scribbled

on one side. "I've got the computer," he said, hurrying after David.

"Yea," David said. "I've got a computer class and have to get online."

Xander said, "Not in our control center, dude. It's only for things that will help find Mom."

"We only have one computer," David complained.

"Tough."

They had reached the top of the stairs. David called over the banister, "Dad! Can I use the computer for school?"

"We'll see," Dad called back.

David yelled, "We only have one!" He showed Xander a sour face.

Xander scowled back at him and leaned close. He whispered, "We only have one mom."

It felt like a punch to David's stomach. He frowned and carried the dry-marker board toward the room that would become their control center. As he was leaving, Xander caught him by the arm.

"I'm sorry," he said.

David looked at the floor. "You can *try* not to be mean, you know."

"I'll try." Xander punched him gently in the shoulder, on the uninjured side.

David stomped him on the foot and ran down the hall, laughing.

Over the next half hour, David, Xander, and Dad carried boxes up to the room. Toria followed them with a notepad. As they thought of things they needed, they called them out to her: bulletin boards, index cards, dry-erase board markers, pushpins, Sharpie markers in different colors, binders, a first aid kit.

Xander thought the computer needed upgrading. "For sure a bigger hard drive and flat-screen monitor," he said. "Maybe *two* screens."

David thought it would be cool to link the notes they would make about each world with possible connections to other worlds or things. He imagined an index card about his time in the French village during WWII linking somehow—he didn't know how yet—to Xander's adventure in the Colosseum.

He asked Toria to add colored string to the list.

Dad dug into the boxes from his days as a teacher and found a time line of all the major events in history. Only a foot tall, it ran some thirty feet long. He mounted it high up along two walls in the mission control center—or MCC, as they were already calling it.

To David, it was the coolest thing so far. After all, the portals apparently were doorways into the past. That got him thinking. He said, "Dad, do the portals ever take you to the future?"

"Not that I've seen, Dae," Dad said, rummaging through a box. They were all in the old servants' quarters now, cleaning, unpacking, setting things up.

"Why not?"

"I don't know. Maybe it has to do with the laws of time travel, or . . ." He shrugged. "Whatever."

"There was that antechamber with things that looked like they were for space travel," Xander said. "Remember, Dae?"

David nodded. "But people do that now," he said.

"Neil Armstrong walked on the moon in 1969," Dad reminded them.

"The *moon?*"

The way Xander said it made David's stomach squirm. Dad scowled at Xander and pointed a finger at him. "Stay away from the rooms with space stuff. At least for now."

"Well, the portals do take you to different times and *places,*" Xander said. "We'll need a big wall map of the world."

"I think I have one," Dad said.

"My string-connection idea is gonna work perfect," David said.

As they became more involved in the task, ideas for making it more useful struck each of them like beads of water in a storm.

Xander said he would draw up a large chart of the hall-way and antechambers. They would write down the items they found in each and keep doing it as the rooms shifted and the items changed. "Maybe there's a pattern to the way they move around that we haven't noticed yet," he said.

"We can link your lists of items to the worlds they lead to, to the map and time line," David said.

Dad added, "So we'll have links from rooms to items, to

historical times, to geographic locations." His grin stretched wide, and he nodded. "This is gonna work. I know it."

David caught his excitement. He said, "Whatever's happening, whoever's behind it—they haven't seen anything like *us* before."

"We'll take 'em by storm," Xander said. "We'll be Bruce Willis in *Die Hard*."

David added, "Aragorn in *Lord of the Rings*."

"Aragorn?" Xander said. "No, no . . . Legolas."

"You're both wrong," Dad said. "Gandalf!"

"I know," David said. "Arnold Schwarzenegger in *Terminator!*"

Xander's eyes got big. In his best deep voice, he said, "I'll be back," and ran out the door.

CHAPTER

twenty-nine

They listened to Xander's footsteps pounding down the hall—toward their bedroom, David thought. But in that house you could never be sure where any sound came from. It was unsettling, like detecting the faint smell of smoke without ever finding out what was causing it.

Toria said, "Dad, did you say flip chart?" She was consulting her list, tapping it with the tip of a mechanical pencil.

"And a stand for it," Dad agreed. "It's like a big tripod."

"For what?" David asked.

"Rules. We'll start a list and refine them as we learn more."

David wrinkled his nose. "Rules? Like what?"

Dad came off the step stool he had been using to reach the time line and smooth out a section. He sat down on the stool. "I've been thinking about this." He held up two fingers. "Two kinds of rules: one are things that we impose on ourselves for safety and to learn the most about the worlds."

"Like the buddy system?" David asked.

"And that we always debrief within an hour of coming back from a world."

"Debrief? What's that?"

"It's sharing everything you learned from a mission—writing about it, talking about it—so you and others can learn from it. If we do it right away, we won't forget anything."

"Like what?"

"Take your trip yesterday to World War II. I'm sure there are things you've already forgotten: what people looked like, any signs that you saw, exactly what you did and the order in which you did it."

David shook his head. "How would any of that help?"

"Until we know what we're dealing with, *anything* could help. What if we realize that we're seeing the same people in different worlds?" He gave David a look that said, *Yeah, huh? What about that?*

David felt something in his head pull painfully tight, like getting a charley horse, but in his mind. He said, "The same people in different worlds? You mean like *us*?"

"Travelers like we are, maybe . . . or not." He looked at David's bewildered face. "Never mind. What I'm saying is, we just don't know what we'll learn once we start recording our experiences, comparing them to each other. That's what debriefing will let us do."

David sat on the floor and leaned his back against the wall. "And debriefing is a *rule*?"

"Well, yes. It's SOP—standard operating procedure. Rules that we implement to help us reach our goal and keep us all on the same page. Like the rule that we never talk about what we're doing here to anyone else. And not to each other in public. And never over the phone. Things like that." He stood and started to pace. "I can think of dozens. We need to write them down and all agree to them."

"Okay," David said, letting out a weak laugh. "I get it. Lots of rules."

"Those are just *our* rules," Dad said. "Then there are the rules of the worlds, the time ripple or whatever it is." He looked at the room around him. "The house."

"The house has rules?" David said.

"The same way everything does," Dad said. "Like the rules of gravity and physics." He leaned over and touched David's bruised cheek. "You cut yourself, you bleed, right?"

"The house doesn't *bleed*."

Dad raised his eyebrows. "As far as we know. But it does do weird things with sound, right? And it doesn't like to have the doors upstairs locked. The antechamber won't change as long as someone's in it or in the world beyond. These are all 'rules,' and I'll bet there are many more we don't even know about yet. We need to make a list of them so we know what we're dealing with, what we can do and what we can't do. Maybe we'll see a pattern that will help us figure this whole thing out."

Dad paced to the end of the room, turned, and came back. "And I think we should try to understand the reason for each rule in the first place."

David lowered his face into his hands. "You're making my head hurt."

"No, Dae, this is good. For example, why can't you bring a camcorder into another world and film your time there?"

David thought about Xander's camcorder that had dangled around his neck the entire time he was playing keep-away from hungry tigers. When he'd come back, all that had been recorded was static. He said, "How are we supposed to find out why the camera didn't work?"

Dad spread out his hands. "I don't know! But that's part of what we're doing here, part of what this room, the MCC, is all about, right? Figuring stuff out, maybe even conducting experiments to learn more."

David frowned. "Experiments" made him think of science class and failing more times than succeeding. He was already trying to get his head around "rules"—two sets of them!—and the very idea that this control center was an attempt to understand something that to David was not understandable: you've got a house with doorways to other times and places, people from those places who can step through and take your mom, and doors that can apparently shake off the locks you put on them—how could you *understand* any of that?

Dad started tapping his chin, thinking. He said, "Let's get a big wall calendar too. We can—"

"How do you spell *calendar*?" Toria asked.

Dad told her, then continued: "It'll help us keep track of what we've already done, how long everything takes to do."

"Like what?" David said.

"Like . . ." Dad thought for a moment. "Like we came to Pinedale on August 13. We found this house the next day."

Because you knew about it before we even started looking, David thought. Instead of rubbing it in, he said, "And we moved in a few days later."

"Right," Dad agreed. "The seventeenth. Last Wednesday."

"Just last Wednesday," David repeated to himself. He could not believe how much had happened since then. It felt like months.

Dad said, "And three days later, yesterday—" He stopped.

David finished for him: "Yesterday morning is when Mom got kidnapped."

Dad shook his head. "So quickly . . ."

Xander rushed into the room, out of breath and holding

an armful of white tubes. David recognized them as rolled movie posters.

"Check it out," Xander said. He dropped the posters on the floor and selected one, then smoothed it open against a bare spot of wall. It displayed a fierce warrior flexing his torso and arms of rippling muscles, gritting his teeth and obviously ready to fight.

"*300?*" David said. "What's that got to do with—"

"Think about it," Xander said. He flashed a big grin over his shoulder. "We're going to be heading into worlds that so far haven't been very friendly to us. We need *guts!* We need to be ready to *fight!* Doesn't this psych you up for that?" He released the poster, which snapped back into a roll, and snatched up another one. He spread it out against the wall.

"*Gladiator!*" David announced: Russell Crowe looking bad and ready to take on the world.

"Yeah?" Xander said, nodding his head with enthusiasm.

"I don't know," Dad said. He was studying the poster with narrow eyes, as though judging a science fair project.

"We can play some music too," Xander said. "I've got tons of soundtracks. Stuff that will really get your blood pumping, you know? We can get one of those clock radios you connect your iPod to. Toria, put that on your list."

She scribbled it down.

Xander nodded toward the posters. "I got *Commando, Die Hard, Matrix* . . ."

"I like where you're going with this," Dad said. He was using his teacher voice. "What bothers me is"—he put his finger on Russell Crowe's breastplate—"we're not these people. We don't have their training, their physical attributes . . ."

"That's not the point, Dad!" Xander said. "These help us get jazzed up for going over. *Mentally*, we're these guys. We're ready! We're tough! We can do it!"

Dad nodded but said, "I understand the mental part. I just don't want us to go diving headlong into a situation we're not ready for."

"All right, look," Xander said. He released the poster and quick-stepped to the far end of the room. "How about if right here"—he turned in a circle, indicating the floor under him—"we *train* to be like those guys? We get in physical shape, and we learn whatever skills we might need in whatever world we're heading to."

Dad shook his head. "Xander—"

Xander cut him off. "Dad! Even if I never learned how to wield a sword or hold a shield, just having the never-say-die warriors of *300* on my mind would have made me better at fighting that gladiator in the Colosseum. Maybe if you hadn't rescued me, I could have fought him off long enough to have found my own way back home, I don't know. But I do know soldiers in war get psyched up like this."

"And soccer players," David chimed.

"Right, athletes!" Xander said. "You're a history teacher. You've studied war. You told me once that battles are won in the mind long before they're won on the battlefield. Isn't *this* what you meant?"

Dad walked to where Xander stood on the other side of the room and looked around, as if trying to see it with Xander's eyes. After a time he smiled and nodded, then said, "Toria, put free weights and exercise mats on the list. Xander, get those posters up on the wall. David, don't you have some killer video game posters?"

David jumped up. "*Halo, Metroid, Call of Duty.*"

"Do they make you want to kick some butt?"

"Oh, yeah!"

"Go get 'em." Dad clapped his hands together. "Come on, guys, let's do this!"

CHAPTER

MOTHER OF MERCY NURSING HOME

Jesse Wagner fidgeted in his wheelchair. He looked at the clock for the thousandth time. Where was Keal? If anyone there would listen to him, it was Keal. To most of the staff at Mother of Mercy, he was just an old man. Heck, he was just an old man to the other old men and women who frittered away their final days in that depressing place. But Keal Jackson was different; he treated people with respect. He was an attendant at the home and knew who still had a light burning in the attic and who didn't.

Shafts of light from sodium vapor lamps in the parking lot streamed through the dirty windows of the community room. Little flecks of dust floated in the light like tiny insects with nowhere to go and nothing to do.

But Jesse did have something to do. Trouble was, he had no way of doing it. Not alone, not by himself. It'd been decades since he could walk without a cane, and eight years now that he'd needed a wheelchair.

He hunched over to stare at his slippered feet. "What good are you?" he yelled at them. "Can't keep a body standing. Can't even shuffle one in front of the other. What good are you!"

A booming voice came from behind him: "You talking to yourself again, Jesse?"

Finally!

Jesse straightened and craned his head around. He said, "'Bout time, Keal. I been waiting for you since yesterday! Don't you work anymore?"

"Gotta have a day off sometime," Keal answered. He came around and dropped into the sagging, cracked vinyl chair in front of Jesse. "Stop being such a grouch." He smiled, a creepy, Cheshire cat thing straight out of *Alice in Wonderland*. The man's skin was so dark, all Jesse's aged vision could make out were Keal's eyes and teeth.

Jesse leaned forward to place a shaky hand on top of Keal's

and gave the attendant his most intent stare, trying to appear as serious and urgent as the task for which he needed Keal's help.

Keal misread the expression. "You suffering from gas today, Jesse?"

"No!" Jesse yelled in his loudest voice, which wasn't loud at all these days. The nurse at the desk in the corner didn't even look up from her magazine. He snatched his hand away and flapped it at the big black man. "I've got urgent business, Keal! Life-and-death business!"

"You don't say." Keal leaned forward.

Jesse sighed with exaggeration. "Listen to me," he said, taking time to make his words clear and strong sounding. "You've known me for what, six years?"

Keal nodded. "Since I started here."

"Have you ever seen me lose my grip on reality? Have I ever rambled about dragons the way ol' Charlie Hobbs used to, God rest his soul? Have I ever thought the cafeteria was a sandy beach in Hawaii, the way Mrs. Thompson does?" He shook his head. "Always taking off her shoes and trying to hang ten on the tables. Have you ever had to restrain me because I thought the night nurses had come to kill me like . . . well, like half the people here? Have you seen me do *anything* crazy?"

Keal flashed his teeth at Jesse again. "I always said you got it together better than most of the staff, Jesse. I hope I'm half as aware when I'm your age . . . if I ever get to be your age."

"So you got to listen to me now, Keal. I mean it. I ain't crazy, even though what I have to say will make me sound that way. Give me the benefit of the doubt, okay?"

Keal's teeth vanished, and the whites of his eyes narrowed. Jesse knew he was frowning.

Good, he thought. *He's listening.*

"I need you to take me somewhere," Jesse said. "Someplace important."

"Like . . . where? If it's the restroom, Jesse, I got you covered, man. Any farther than that, we got a problem."

"California," Jesse said firmly.

Another flash of teeth, and Keal boomed with laughter. "Oh, Jesse, Jesse . . . you know I can't take the residents outside the building, less'n it's to the hospital, or maybe an occasional field trip to the park."

Jesse let him laugh. When it was all out of Keal, and the aide had caught his breath, Jesse said, "People will die if I don't get there. Lots of people."

He felt Keal's big hand on his knee.

The attendant said, "Jesse . . . I . . . I don't know what to say. You know—"

"I know what I know," Jesse snapped. "I have to get a message to someone, a message so important I have to do it in person. He may not believe me, otherwise. And I have to show him . . ."

"Show him what?"

Jesse closed his eyes. "I have to show him how to . . . to . . ."

He didn't know how to say it differently, but he also knew how it would sound. "I have to show him how to save the world."

"Save the world?"

"I know how it sounds."

It was Keal's turn to sigh. He said, "Who is it you think you have to see?"

"I don't know who, exactly." Jesse shook his head. "I mean, I *do* . . . but . . . but it's been so *long*. It could be almost anyone. No, not *anyone* . . ."

Keal gave his knee a gentle squeeze. "Calm down, Jesse. It's okay. So this guy—whoever he is—he's going to save the world?"

"Yes, yes, but he doesn't know it yet. I have to tell him." He squeezed his eyes closed again. His lungs didn't work the way they used to. He had to pull hard just to get enough air. "His father, or his father's father, was supposed to show him, but I know he didn't. It's been too long. He didn't do what he was supposed to do. He left his post."

"Post? Jesse, I have to say, man, you might as well be ranting about dragons and surfing on the tables, for all the sense you're making."

Jesse gripped Keal's hand in both of his. He squeezed, but knew Keal hardly felt it. "His *post*," he repeated. "The house. They left the house . . . for *years* they left the house." He squinted at the whites of Keal's eyes. "It's not a house you want to leave. It's too special, it's too *important*."

"A house, Jesse?" Keal said. "You're talking about a house?"

"Like no other house, like no other place."

"And that's where you want to go? To this house? In California?"

Jesse pulled in air. He wasn't getting enough. He nodded.

"How do you know about this house, Jesse? Did you live there?"

Jessie smiled at a memory. Then other memories flooded into his head, wiping the smile away. He said, "I more than lived there." He glanced around and leaned closer. Then he whispered, "I built it."

CHAPTER

thirty-one

MONDAY, 7:11 P.M.

Xander King had walked completely around the outside of the house. He had to plow through bushes and scale trees to do it, but he finally managed to film the entire exterior. He planned to upload the footage to their computer and print still pictures of every angle. He imagined a wall of house photos in the war room, David's "MCC."

He stood midway between the house and the dirt road,

where their 4Runner was parked. He squinted up at the second-floor windows above the porch roof and wondered if he should try to get a few close-ups of them. But it was early evening, and he was losing his light. The sun was already gone from the sky, leaving only a reddish-purple glow. Even that was fading fast.

The term "false twilight" came to him. It was when darkness came earlier than it should have, usually from a solar eclipse or because the shadows in a canyon grew dark with the slightest dropping of the sun. The woods around the house were like that, near-black despite the sky's luminance.

He didn't want to be outside much longer. Besides, they'd gotten up early and had to go to school again tomorrow. Dad would want them all to go to bed before too long.

A clatter came from the house. Xander's heart jumped as the front door burst open. Then he recognized David bounding off the porch without touching a single step.

"Xander!" David called.

"What?"

"Dad wants you."

Xander pushed a black cap over the camcorder's lens.

"Now!" David said, insistent.

"Hold your—" He registered the urgency on David's face. He brushed past him, heading for the door. "What is it? Is he all right?"

"He went through," David said. "He's in a world!"

Xander stopped to look at his brother. "What? Why? Did he see Mom?"

"No. We were cleaning up the locks upstairs. He looked in one of the rooms and laughed. He said he remembered it from when he was a kid and wanted to show it to you. He said he was going on ahead and told me to come get you."

"Why me? Why not you?"

"He said I can go later."

David pushed him, and Xander hurried up the porch steps.

David continued: "He said he'd been wanting to talk to you, and this was the perfect place."

"He went on alone?" Xander couldn't believe it. "Without anyone even in the antechamber?"

"What holds the room in place, he said, was being in the *world*, not the antechamber." David added: "I propped the door open with a picnic basket. Just in case."

They went through the door, and Xander pushed it closed.

"Lock it," David said. "Dad wants to keep the house battened down." He smiled. "That's what he said: *battened down.*"

They started up the stairs.

Xander said, "Where's Toria?"

"Playing in her room. I'll wait for you guys in the antechamber."

In the second-floor hallway, heading for the hidden stairwell, Xander stopped again. He turned to David. "Did you say *picnic basket?*"

....

Xander's sneakered feet stepped onto the softness of tall grass. A light breeze blew past. The air felt warm, but he saw no sun in the sky, just a uniform pinkish glow. Dawn or dusk, he couldn't tell. Thin tendrils of clouds swooped in long arcs, as though fingers had raked across the sky. He looked over his shoulder to see the wavering image of David standing in the little room. Then the door slammed shut without a sound. The image broke apart like dandelion fluff and disappeared.

He reached up to tug at the rim of the wool cap he'd taken from a hook in the antechamber. It was checkered, with a little pom-pom on the top, like ones he'd seen some serious golfers wear. At his hip, hanging by a strap over his shoulder, was the picnic basket David had told him about. It was empty, but that didn't stop it from helping him unlock the portal door. In his left hand he carried a net at the end of a yard-long pole. SpongeBob used one like it to catch jellyfish; Xander had had no idea it was something people actually owned.

Scoping out his surroundings, he started to understand the items. He was standing in a meadow at the top of a gentle hill. The grass rose as high as his knees. It swayed one way and then the other, reminding him of rolling swells in the open ocean. Wildflowers swirled among the grass: white and yellow, blue and red. Butterflies fluttered over the petals. Several flitted past him on their way from one patch of flowers to another. As far as he could see, the land around him rose and fell like a rumpled blanket. Woods occupied some of the space, covering one hill but not another.

Movement at the edge of the meadow caught his eye. A family of deer stepped from the shadows of trees. A buck with huge antlers stepped forward, studied Xander, then stooped to chew on the grass.

At the bottom of the gently sloping meadow, a river ran across the pristine landscape. It was about a mile away, but he could see his father sitting on a blanket near the glistening ribbon of water. He was leaning back on one arm and tossing something over the grassy bank into the river.

Xander started down the hill. From the woods, birds chirped. He heard an eagle's cry and looked up to see two of the majestic birds sailing in circles overhead. More animals—a fox, a couple of rabbits, a coyote—ventured from different places in the woods. They sniffed the air, looked at Xander, then went about their business. None seemed concerned by his presence.

He filled his lungs. The air tasted *fresh*, like it contained more oxygen than he was used to. He wondered if he was high up. The Rockies, maybe or . . . what were the other big mountain ranges? The Alps, the Himalayas, the Andes . . . But he didn't see any of the jagged, snowcapped peaks he would expect if he were in any of those places.

He could hear the river now. The water rushed over rocks, poured over short drop-offs.

His father looked relaxed. He sat with one knee cocked up, the other leg stretched out before him. While Xander watched, he turned his head, appeared to select a pebble from the ground beside the blanket, and casually tossed it into the water.

"Hey!" Xander called.

Dad looked back over his shoulder and waved.

Xander spread his arms out. "What *is* this?"

"Nice, huh?"

Xander set the net and picnic basket down. He dropped onto the blanket. His dad tossed another pebble, and Xander followed it with his eyes. He watched the water rushing by, tumbling and churning. He realized that flowing water could be as complicated and interesting to watch as flames. The two shared a kind of orderly chaos.

He said, "I don't get it."

"What don't you get?"

"This." Xander looked around. "I thought all the worlds were violent and dangerous."

"Most are," Dad said. "In fact, this is the only one my father found that wasn't like that."

"So why's it here? What's it about?"

Dad shook his head slowly. "Maybe it's a respite from the insanity of the other worlds, a peaceful break. Grandpa thought of it that way. I think this was one of the reasons he gave up the search and took us away."

That jolted Xander. "*This* place? I thought it was the dangers of the other worlds that made him think he would go crazy. Or that he thought he'd die and leave you and Aunt Beth alone in the house. Or that someone would take you and—"

Dad nodded. "Those things were the raging storms he weathered every day. *This*—" He took in the landscape around him, a satisfied smile on his lips. "This was his break from those horrors."

"So why would it drive him away?"

Dad looked at him from the corner of his eyes. "Because he was afraid he'd come here and stay."

Xander thought about that. He said, "Wow."

"If he didn't have other responsibilities—kids—maybe he would have done just that."

"And no one would ever know," Xander said. He found a pebble and tossed it in. "It *is* nice."

"When I looked in the antechamber and saw the items—the basket and blanket—" He nodded at the cap Xander wore. "The tam-o'-shanter."

"So that's what it's called." Xander touched the pom-pom and smiled.

"Snazzy," Dad said, winking. "When I saw them, I remembered the world that lay beyond. My father took me here a couple of times. I wanted you to see it."

"Yeah, why me? David was with you."

Dad watched the river. His face was expressionless. Finally he said, "Because as much as David loves Mom and misses her, he doesn't blame himself for her being gone."

"*What?*" Xander snapped, surprised. "You think I blame myself? If anybody, I blame—"

"Me. I know." Dad looked directly into his eyes. "But I think you believe you should have stopped that man."

"I . . ." Xander started.

But Dad was right. Xander had never admitted it even to himself, but his inability to stop the man from taking Mom had been haunting him. He felt shame and anger at himself.

Dad patted Xander on the knee. "You have every right to be mad at me. I don't blame you, and I'm not going to tell you to feel otherwise. Not about me. But you did everything you could to help her. That man was twice your size and experienced at doing what he did. You can't punish yourself for not stopping him."

Dad blurred in Xander's vision, and he thought the portal was materializing right there between them. Then he realized that tears had filled his eyes. He blinked, spilling them down his cheeks.

Dad turned to press his body to Xander and wrap his arm around his neck. Xander expected him to say again how sorry he was, but Dad simply held him. After a few moments, Xander lowered his head and cried on his father's shoulder.

He let it all come out, all the sorrow and fear he'd been trying to pretend he didn't feel. When it was over, he straightened. He saw that he'd soaked Dad's shoulder. He laughed a little and brushed at it.

Dad's eyes were red too. "I wanted . . ." he said. His voice broke, and he had to stop. He pulled in a couple deep breaths, then said, "I wanted you to see this so you'd know it isn't all bad. Your mother could be somewhere like this."

"You believe that?" Xander said.

Dad nodded thoughtfully. He studied Xander's face. He said, "You look so much like her."

Xander wiped the back of his hand under his nose. "But *am* I like her?"

"You mean independent, resourceful, tenacious? Oh, yeah."

Xander chuckled. He pushed the wetness out of his eye sockets. "This family is way too weepy," he said.

Dad pointed at him. "No more of that!" He sniffed and slapped Xander's knee, then stood. "Come on. We'd better get back."

"I can feel it," Xander said. "The pull."

"The more sensitive you are to it, the better."

"But I'm not feeling it this way," Xander said. "It's tugging me back toward where I stepped into this world."

"Me too," Dad said. "I just want to do one thing first." They headed for a big tree.

"Dad?" Xander asked, watching his sneakers kick down the

footlong blades of grass. "Why did this happen? I mean, why did God *let* this happen?"

His father stopped. He gave Xander a long, serious look. "I don't know, Son. But I trust that He has His reasons."

"You *trust*? After He let Mom get taken?"

Dad bit his lip, thinking. Finally, he touched his chest. "It's here. I don't know how to explain it."

Xander shook his head. Whatever it was Dad felt, it wasn't the same in Xander.

Dad gripped his shoulder and gave it a squeeze. "Give it time, Xander. You'll see."

"I doubt it."

They stood like that for a while, then continued their trek to the big tree. Dad produced a pocketknife and unfolded it. He began scraping the point against the bark.

"What are you doing?" Xander asked.

"You know when we were talking about your mother leaving notes in our lunches?"

The mark on the tree started taking on a shape Xander recognized. "Sure."

Without pausing the blade, Dad said, "That got me thinking. I'm leaving a note for *her*."

It was "Bob," the cartoon face both parents often doodled on notes and cards to each other and the kids. Xander sometimes found the face on a scrap of paper among his homework paper or stuck in his shoe. It told him someone was thinking about him. Dad said it had started with Grandpa Hank, and Dad had scribbled it since he was a kid.

Xander said, "Bob?"

"Bob," Dad confirmed, starting on the bulbous, heavily lidded eyes. "It'll let her know we're looking for her, that we've been here."

"But no one else will know it's from us or to her," Xander concluded.

"Exactly," Dad said. "You never know when a message could cause problems. If no one else recognizes it as a message, it won't stir anything up."

"Except in Mom."

Dad stepped back to appraise his handiwork: one goofy face carved in a tree trunk.

"Will it stay?" Xander asked.

"Stay?"

"I mean after we're gone. Does time get weird here? Will it suddenly be the past and Bob will never have been here, or will it become the future and Bob will be long gone?"

Dad scowled at him. "I never thought of that." He looked at Bob. "I don't know."

"I hope he stays," Xander said. "I want her to know we're looking for her."

Dad folded up the knife and dropped it into his pocket. He put his arm around Xander's shoulder and steered him toward the portal, according to the pull of the antechamber items. "She knows we are, Xander. Even without Bob, she knows."

CHAPTER

thirty-two

Monday, 8:05 p.m.

David sat on the bench in the antechamber, backstroking with one arm. His right hand rose up and descended, palm down as though pushing water past his body. His left elbow rose as far as the sling would allow. In his mind, he finished the stroke. Then the process started all over again with his right hand rising above his head.

He watched the door Dad and Xander had gone through. His

eyes flicked to the other door, the one that led to the hallway and the rest of the house. He'd been hearing noises for some time now: creaking floorboards, thuds. Once he thought he heard a door slam. It was nearby, one of the other doors on that floor. Then there was the telephone downstairs. Every few minutes, it would ring and ring and ring. *Why didn't Toria answer it?*

His mouth was dry, and his stomach hurt from rolling over on itself every time he heard a noise or imagined something creeping around in the hallway.

He heard a loud drawing of breath, like someone sucking air in through his teeth. He jumped, staring at the hallway door. Then he realized it was coming from the other door, the portal door. Air hissed through the gap underneath it. He couldn't tell if it was blowing into the little room or being sucked out of it. The last thing he wanted to do was get close enough to feel for the wind's direction.

Dim light appeared under the door and quickly grew in intensity until it was blindingly bright. Squinting at it, he saw the light trace a line around the entire door. Shadows flickered through the light as though something was moving past the door on the other side. The handle began to turn. David stood and backed into the hallway door.

The portal door burst open. Wind whooshed in, carrying leaves and grass and a meadowy fragrance. The portal itself looked like a churning cauldron of dry ice, backlit by flood lamps. The smoky air swirled around and around. It thinned and blew away, off to either side of the door. In its place was an out-of-focus image of greens and browns. The colors shifted and came together, forming a human figure.

Xander stepped into the room, coming down hard on his feet as though stepping off a foot-high platform. He fell to the floor, grunting.

David fell to his knees beside him. "Xander! You all right?"

Xander raised his head. His hair was a mess. There was a leaf stuck in it. "Yeah," he said. "Gotta remember to watch that first step. It's a doozy."

"Where's Dad?" David said. He looked through the portal just as another figure formed out of the colors.

Xander rolled out of the way as Dad came crashing through: "*Oomph!*"

Dad saw Xander beside him and touched him. "You all right?"

"Took you long enough," David said.

Dad swung around to him. "What's wrong?"

"I've been hearing noises in the hallway, and the phone keeps ringing."

"What noises?"

"I heard creaking, and a door slammed."

Dad scrambled to his feet. He tossed down the blanket and said, "Xander, put the items back. Let's go."

Halfway to the staircase, the phone began ringing again.

Dad said, "David——?"

"Got it!" David ran ahead, clomped down the stairs and into

the master bedroom. Toria was sitting on the bed, an array of dolls and their clothes splayed across the bedspread. The phone on the nightstand started into its fourth ring.

"Why didn't you answer it?" David said.

"I'm not supposed to."

David snatched up the wireless receiver and thumbed a button. "Hello?"

"There you are. Mr. King. I need to speak to Mr. King." The woman's words rattled at him, fast as machine-gun fire.

"One moment, please." He ran into the hall and met his father coming through the secret panel in the wall. He held the phone out to him.

"Sounds important," David whispered.

Dad put the phone to his face. "Hello? . . . Yes?" He continued down the hall.

David turned to Xander. In a hushed voice he said, "It sounded like my homeroom teacher, Mrs. Moreau."

Xander made a face. "What did you do?"

"Nothing. It wasn't me, it was that kid I told you about. Clayton. She sent him to the office."

"Boys!" Dad called. He had walked around the corner into the main upstairs hallway. Now he stepped back into view. "Come on! We gotta go!"

"Where?" Xander said.

Dad vanished again, his footsteps clumping away. "City hall. Toria, grab your shoes."

"City hall? Why?" Xander called as the brothers raced around the corner.

Dad came out of the master bedroom, pulling their sister along by the hand. His face was tight with worry. He said, "Someone's trying to take the house!"

thirty-three

MONDAY, 8:37 P.M.

In the 4Runner, Dad explained that someone had claimed that
the house was unsafe. "The town council convened an emergency meeting to consider evicting us."

"Just because someone said our house was unsafe?" Xander
said. His voice was high in disbelief.

"Apparently somebody is trying to convince them that you
guys are in danger," Dad said. "They got the doctor who set

David's arm telling the council about his injuries. Someone's claiming he was hurt in the house because it's so dilapidated."

"What's that?" Toria said.

"Rundown," Xander answered.

"You keep saying *someone*," David said. "Who is someone?"

Dad's eyes caught his in the rearview mirror. "That's what I asked. The woman on the phone said she didn't know."

"Or didn't want to tell you," Xander said.

David thought about the doctor's line of questioning at the clinic. He said, "No one said it was *you* who hurt me?"

Dad shook his head. "Not yet, but that doesn't mean they're not going to. I have a feeling this is just the beginning."

"Or the end," Xander said, "if the city council believes them and kicks us out. Dad, you can't let that happen!"

Dad said, "There's something else I don't get . . . why is this a city council matter? You'd think the safety of children would go to social services or even the police department."

Xander said, "They do things differently in small towns. Do they even *have* social services here?"

"Still, calling in the city council just feels like overkill to me," Dad said. "Like using a nuke when a penknife would do. And why wouldn't they just come out and look for themselves?"

In the rearview mirror David could see his father's brows getting closer together as he thought about it.

Dad said, "I think something bigger is going on."

"Bigger?" Xander said. "Like what?"

Dad just shook his head. He said, "The mayor will probably be there. He was one of the people who interviewed me for my job." His eyes found David in the mirror. "Dae, the woman on the phone hung up when I asked who she was. Any idea?"

Xander spoke up. "He thinks it was his teacher."

"Teacher? Who?"

"Mrs. Moreau," David said.

Xander said, "Dad, what if the phone call was just a way to get us out of the house?"

That made Dad's eyebrows actually touch. He said, "What makes you think that?"

"We saw somebody watching our house last night."

"When?"

"After the thing with the locks. I got up to go to the bathroom."

Dad said, "Maybe it was that Taksidian guy. Why didn't you tell me?"

Xander threw up his hands. "It was late . . . I just thought . . ."

"Listen, guys . . ." Dad shifted his head around to make eye contact with each of his children. His attention returned to the road before he continued: "With all that's going on, *everything* is important. And somebody watching the house!" He scowled at Xander. "How could you think that wasn't important?"

"I didn't say it wasn't important!"

"But you didn't tell me!"

Xander's shoulders slumped. Instead of explaining himself, he turned away to look out the window. David knew what he was thinking: with school, setting up the MCC, Dad and Xander going into another world—when was there time to even *think* of anything else? Maybe it was this kind of thing that the control room was meant for, a place to record things and keep everything straight. He knew Dad was right. With so much at stake, everything was important.

"Here we go." Dad said, braking to a hard stop.

They were on Pinedale's main street in front of the city hall. The front doors were open and people were coming out, descending the stairs, talking to one another. They all seemed to notice Dad at the same time. David thought they were trying not to look guilty of something.

Dad opened the door and hopped out. He beelined it for an older man who was halfway down the concrete steps.

Xander unsnapped his seat belt and swiveled around to face Toria and David. "That's the mayor. His picture was on the wall in one of my classes."

David said, "His picture? Weird."

"Welcome to Pinedale." Xander opened his door and scrambled out.

David and Toria did the same. They all came together on the steps around Dad and the mayor. The other people who had come out of the building were watching from safe distances in both directions of the street.

Dad was saying, " . . . this isn't right, and you know it."

The mayor said, "Now, Ed, our only concern is for the children."

The way he spoke made David think of a glazed doughnut, all soft and sugary.

The mayor glanced at each of the King kids in turn. He paused on David, taking in, David was sure, his black eye, bruised cheek, and broken arm. Turning back to Dad, he said, "When we get reports like this, of course we have to investigate."

"Reports like what?" Dad snapped.

"Well . . . uh . . ." His hand rose to indicate David.

Dad continued: "I think *investigation* is the right word here. But it sounds to me like you've already investigated—or have no intention of ever investigating."

"Ed, we *know* that house. It's been rundown for years."

"So?" Dad's volume rose a notch. "That doesn't automatically make it unsafe. Are you questioning my judgment when it comes to keeping my family safe? I can't believe all these people are going along with this." Dad looked around at the men and women who were watching from the sidewalk.

Suddenly he froze, and David saw the muscles in his jaw tighten, his eyes narrow. He looked over his shoulder to follow his father's gaze. David's heart jumped into his throat.

Across the street, in an alleyway between two stores, stood a man. Though the figure was partially hidden by shadows, the light from a streetlamp crossed over his face, revealing Taksidian. As David watched, the man took a step back and vanished in the darkness.

"Oh, I see," Dad said. "Tell me, Steve, did your report happen to come from Mr. Taksidian?"

The mayor swallowed, his eyes darting to the people standing around. He said, "It was . . . uh . . . anonymous. But I'll have you know, Mr. Taksidian means a lot to this town. He is considering relocating several of his businesses to Pinedale. What that means to us, economically, at a time when businesses have been closing, people moving away—"

Dad held up his palm. "I get it," he said. His hand became a pointing finger aimed directly at the mayor's nose. "Let me tell you. Whatever you do, make sure you can support it in a court of law, because that's where you're going to end up."

For just a moment the mayor's eyes focused on Dad's finger. He actually looked frightened—though David thought something like *I'll hunt you down like a dog* would have worked better.

The mayor composed himself and said, "Mr. King, is that a threat?"

Dad's finger didn't waver. David was awfully glad it wasn't pointed at him.

"I'm just telling you, Steve, don't mess with me, my family, or my house." Dad turned and descended a few steps toward the car.

The mayor cleared his throat and said, "Speaking of your family, Ed, where is the missus? We heard another report that—"

Dad spun around, and his index finger came up again. "Don't mess with us. I mean it," he warned. "Come on, kids."

He climbed into the SUV and slammed the door.

David ran around and was the last one in. The car pulled forward before he had his door shut. As they drove past, David looked hard into the alley where Taksidian had stood, but the man was gone, leaving only darkness.

thirty-four

MONDAY, 11:57 P.M.

That night, the day's events kept replaying in David's head. He was exhausted, but he wasn't sure he'd ever again get a good night's rest. Even being in his own bed didn't help. *If you can't turn off your thoughts,* he said to himself, *who cares how soft your pillow is?*

Xander's whispered voice reached him from out of the darkness: "You awake?"

"Yeah," he whispered back. He looked over toward

Xander's bed. The moonlight coming through the windows was enough to show his brother sitting up. He looked at the clock on the nightstand. "Almost the witching hour," he said.

"No such thing," Xander told him.

"I'm not sure about anything anymore," David said. "What's real, what's not . . . this house has confused everything."

When Xander didn't say anything, David realized he had been hoping his brother would laugh at his words, say they were crazy. He wanted somebody to tell him the world was essentially the same as he thought it was before coming to Pinedale, but it wasn't. Their mom was gone, and they lived in a house that messed with time and space. The past was supposed to be the past—unreachable, unchangeable. Here, however, things that belonged in history books were as easy to get to as the bathroom.

See? he thought. *Thinking again. Why can't I let it all go, at least until morning?*

Xander said, "I've been thinking."

"Join the club. I can't turn it off."

"No, listen." Xander shifted from his bed to David's. "They're trying to take our house or kick us out or something."

"I know," David said. "It's that Taksidian guy."

"It doesn't even matter who's behind it. If they kick us out, who knows what will happen? They'll probably chain the doors, board up all the windows. Maybe even tear the whole place down."

David sat up and scooted back against the headboard. "They can't do that. It's our house."

"Dad Googled Taksidian. He's some rich bigwig. Owns all these companies. People like that can do anything they want."

"Not *anything*," David said. This was another way the world was not as David had always imagined. Maybe it didn't involve ripples in time or monsters, but it was equally scary.

"Just about," Xander said. "Don't you think a man like that can take any house he wants?"

David thought about it. With enough money and lawyers, dishonesty and meanness, of course he could. David's chest felt tight.

"What—" he started to say, then realized how close he was to crying. He took a deep breath and tried again. "What's going to happen to Mom?"

"That's what I've been thinking about," Xander said. "The MCC is cool, but Dad's taking too long. He's so concerned about appearances and keeping people off our backs so we have all the time in the world to find Mom . . ." He shook his head. "But we don't *have* all the time in the world. We may not even have a few days."

"There's nothing we can do about that, Xander."

"We can start looking for Mom *now*. Forget playing it safe. Forget debriefings and motivational seminars. We gotta just do it, Dae. We gotta find Mom."

"What are you saying?"

Xander leaned closer. He squeezed David's leg. "Come with me! Now!"

"What, just . . . *go over?*"

"Between the two of us, we can cover the same ground in half the time."

"Xander, I don't know. I promised Dad I wouldn't."

"Come on, David, what do we have to lose?"

"Our *lives?*"

"Think about it. The faster we go, the more worlds we see, the better chance we have to find Mom."

This is it, David thought. As much as he wanted to find Mom, as much as he'd gone along with setting up the control room and making plans for searching through the various worlds, somewhere inside he had hoped it would not be necessary. Maybe Mom would just show up. Or Dad would decide that he was too young.

The first time he went over, he had almost been killed by tigers and tribesmen with spears. The second time, he had almost been killed by Nazis. Two times through, two close calls. He didn't like those odds. They had cured him of his desire for that kind of adventure.

He looked at the clock again. It was exactly midnight. With far less enthusiasm than usual, he said, "Let's do it."

CHAPTER

thirty-five

"Why are they shooting at me?" David screamed.

There was a *crack!* in the distance, and the earth beside him erupted in a mini-geyser of dirt. They had stepped into a nightmare battlefield where bodies littered the ground, the injured howled in pain, and David had become a target before drawing his third breath. Though Xander and he were near each other, it was clear the shooters wanted David. One man who had aimed a rifle at him lowered it when Xander darted into the line of fire. That did not stop others from plugging away at him.

"Get down! Get down!" Xander said, waving his arms at David. Xander was sidestepping in circles around his brother, trying to spot and dissuade the next would-be shooter. It seemed every time he circled around one way, a shot rang out from the opposite direction, and a bullet would sail past so closely they could hear it, or it would hit the ground at their feet.

A thick plume of smoke drifted past, hiding Xander from David's view. David panicked. "Xander! Xander!"

"I'm here, Dae, stay down."

David felt warm wetness on his cheeks and thought for sure he had been hit. He wiped at it. Only tears, and they were flowing as heavily as blood would have from a head wound. He dropped to his hands and knees and yelled again, "Why are they shooting at me?"

The smoke cleared. Xander was standing ten feet away. "Your uniform!" he said. "David, your uniform."

David looked at the jacket he had put on in the antechamber. One side was draped over his cast. It was gray, like the kepi he wore on his head. To gain passage into this world, he had also carried a rifle. Xander had recognized it from *Glory, The Patriot,* and other Civil War movies: it was a Harper's Ferry rifle, single shot and muzzle loaded. He had confirmed that it was unloaded, with the gunpowder and musket ball nowhere in the antechamber.

"All the better," Xander had said. "You'd end up shooting your foot off, or worse, shooting me."

David had forgotten all about it as soon as the first bullet zinged past his head.

He looked up from the gray wool of his uniform to see that Xander was wearing dark blue. In his hand, he held a sword—the only other weapon in the room after David had gotten dibs on the rifle.

"They think you're a Confederate soldier, David!" Xander yelled. He glanced around. "We're on the Union side of the battle." He looked back at David and saw something that made his eyes grow even wider. "And you've got that rifle! Throw it away! David, throw the rifle away!"

David heaved it off to the side.

A shot rang out, then another. Dirt kicked up into his face. Another round passed so closely over his head he thought for sure it had taken off his kepi, if not his scalp. He reached up and felt the soft cloth of the worn hat. He spat dirt out of his mouth. "*Xander!*" he screamed with everything he had in him.

"Lie down! Lie down!" Xander yelled, running to him.

David did, and Xander lay down on top of him. Xander's breaths were loud and quick in his ear. David couldn't help it: his weeping became full-out crying.

"I told you . . . I told you," he repeated. It was all he could say, over and over.

"Shhh," Xander whispered into his ear. "It's going to be okay."

Nearby, the ground exploded. Hurled into the air was a thousand times more dirt than the musket balls had kicked up.

"What . . . what . . . what . . ." David screamed, pulling in a short breath between each word.

"Cannonball," Xander said. "I think the Confederates are advancing. We can't stay here."

When David had awakened that morning with the first day of school on his mind, it had never occurred to him that he would die that same night in the dirt by a Union soldier's musket ball. He squeezed his eyes closed. He tried not to think about the rifle fire and the screams, the smoke that stung his nostrils and scorched his throat.

He forced himself to think of home. He would have liked to have tasted Toria's meat loaf, to have kicked the mayor of Pinedale in the shin, to have used their mission control center at least once. That got him thinking about something he wanted to write on Dad's flip chart: *What is it about these worlds and WAR?* In his mind, he underlined *WAR* three times. WWII. The Civil War. He would even say Xander's battle with the gladiator was a form of war. What else would you call it when people tried to kill you—whether it was a single person or many—and other people approved.

The chorus of gunfire they had been hearing in the distance grew louder, closer. Another cannonball slammed down, too close for comfort.

"We can't stay here," Xander repeated.

"What are we supposed to do?" David gasped. "As soon as I stand up, they'll shoot me."

Xander was quiet for what seemed like a long time. Finally he said, "I'm sorry I got you into this, Dae."

"I don't want to hear it, Xander," David said. "Don't apologize; just get me home."

Xander squirmed above him, apparently looking for something that would save them.

"Listen, you go, Xander. I'll stay here and play dead."

"I can't do that," Xander said loudly into his ear. "Anything could happen." He paused. Then: "Wait, wait, wait." He rolled off of David and vanished into a wall of drifting smoke.

"Xander!" David rose up onto his elbow. "Xander!" The barrel of a rifle jutted straight toward his face. He screamed and dropped his head into the dirt. He covered himself with his good arm as if it could protect him from a musket load. He wondered if he would hear the gunfire, or if the next thing he heard would be angels welcoming him into heaven.

When neither an explosion nor heavenly voices reached his ears, he lowered his arm and looked up. The opening of the barrel was big and black and six inches in front of his eyes. At the other end stood Xander, staring off to the side. Xander swung his attention back to David.

"Come on!" Xander said, "Didn't you hear me? Get up."

"Xander, what—"

Xander's eyes flicked around, then he said, "Don't say my name. You're my prisoner, understand? That's how we're getting out of here. Let's go."

David fought back a smile. He wiped the sleeve of his trouble-some jacket under his nose, leaving a streak of snot and dirt. He rose and noticed that the other soldiers in blue were moving backwards, firing in the opposite direction. He turned to head the same way, raised his good hand, and began walking.

Behind him Xander said, "Take off your hat so they can see you're just a boy."

David pulled it off and held it above him in his hand.

"Don't hold it up like that," Xander said. "Let's not give anybody a gray target to shoot at."

"Don't we need it to find the portal?"

"Stick it in your belt," Xander instructed.

David lowered his hand to do that. He thought that hav-ing his arm down out of a surrender position made him fair game for anyone who wanted to shoot. He got his hand back in the air as fast as he could. He said, "Xander . . . ?"

"Don't use my name!"

"What if the portal home is on the Confederate side? I'm not feeling the items pull me yet."

Xander said, "Back when I was lying on you, I thought I felt my jacket pulling in this direction. But it might have been the wind . . . or you. Wherever it is, David, we'll get to it. I promise."

David believed his brother. On a list of character traits, Xander's top two would be determination and stubbornness.

David said, "Don't use my name."

CHAPTER

thirty-six

They marched for a long time. They went over one, two, three hills, past the slow-moving injured and those who would never move again. Some soldiers ran by on their way to the front lines. They frowned at David. The anger in their eyes seemed to change to sadness when they registered his age. One man nodded at Xander and said, "Good job, private."

Dutifully, Xander replied, "Thank you, sir."

Finally, tents and groups of scurrying soldiers came into

view. As they drew closer, an older man with a closely cropped black beard broke away from a small group of soldiers to walk toward them. His jacket had a high collar and two rows of brass buttons running down his chest. Patches embroidered with stars were sewn to the top of each shoulder. He stepped in front of David. His eyes roamed down to David's feet, then back to his face.

"How old are you, son?" the man said.

David pulled his jacket closed in front, making sure his cast was hidden. He said, "Twelve, sir."

"And those cur dogs got you fighting?"

David thought fast. He figured an officer wouldn't take kindly to an enemy combatant regardless of age. He said, "No, sir. I'm only a drummer boy."

The officer narrowed his eyes at David. "Caught without your drum?"

David said, "Taken from me, sir."

The man said, "You know what I hear about young recruits?"

"Sir?"

"If they want to fight, they scrawl the number 18 on a piece of paper and put it in their shoe. When enlistment officers ask them if they're 'over eighteen,' they can honestly answer, 'Yes, sir, I am.' Those dogs are so desperate for soldiers, they take them at their word even when they know they're putting a child on the battlefield." The man stepped closer. "What concerns me are all the Southern children who do that in order to put musket balls in my men. You didn't do that, son, did you?"

Every organ in David's body felt shriveled to the size of a pea. It was all he could do to keep from passing out. He said, "No, sir. Just a drummer boy."

The man squinted down at David's sneakers. He said, "Son, those are the strangest shoes I've ever seen."

"Sneak—" David started, then backed up. "I mean, sir, my mother made them."

"No offense to your mama, but I think she could use some lessons."

"Yes, sir."

The man looked past David to Xander. "Oh, no," he said. "How old are *you?*"

"Fif—" Xander's voice suddenly grew deep. "Eighteen, sir."

The man frowned. "Beauregard hit our blind side. What's your take?"

"Pretty bad, sir. We saw . . . uh, *I* saw lots of casualties back there."

The bearded man nodded. He said—more to himself than to Xander, David thought—"Retreat is not dishonorable. *Unnecessary* retreat is. I don't believe it's time to shoot the horse."

"No, sir."

The man scowled at Xander. "You know where the stockade is?" Conveniently, he pointed down the camp's center aisle.

"Yes, sir."

"Carry on, then." The man stepped aside.

David felt the barrel of the rifle poke his spine. His feet felt like they were made of cement, but they moved on down the middle of the encampment.

"What was that 'shoot the horse' stuff?" David whispered.

"I think it's his version of throwing in the towel. Do you know who that was?"

"A guy who almost shot me," David said flatly.

"Ulysses S. Grant."

When David said nothing, Xander went on: "He became president of the United States. He's on the fifty-dollar bill."

Xander seemed more impressed by this last fact than by the first.

David simply nodded. As they moved toward the back of the camp, he finally spoke up. "How come I got the gray uniform?"

"Luck of the draw, Dae." After a few moments, he added, "And I am sorry about this."

"I know." He walked a few paces. "Xander—"

"Don't use my—"

David said, "Xander, Xander, Xander."

Xander sighed and said, "What?"

"I don't see any way we could look for Mom like this. And I just want to go home."

"Yeah," Xander said. "I have an idea. Come on." He grabbed David by the collar and tugged him toward a tent.

"Hey!" David said. "What are you——?"

"Just trying to make it look real. You're my prisoner, remember? Now, *shhh*."

Xander pulled the tent flap back. Past his brother, David saw a man getting dressed. Xander said, "Excuse me." He let the flap fall back into place and pushed David on.

"What are we doing?" David whispered.

"I'm looking for something."

"What?"

But they had reached the flap of the next tent. Xander had his ear close to the canvas, listening. Inside, someone was screaming in pain.

"Xander, let's go to the next one!" David said.

Xander pulled back the flap and gasped. David couldn't keep his eyes from looking. A man lay on a table, convulsing. Blood jutted from a wound in his neck. His screams became gurgles. A woman in what David assumed was a nurse's hat and covered in blood held a cloth to another injury in the man's chest. She looked up quickly.

"Boy!" she yelled. "You must fetch Dr. Scott. Two tents down. Hurry!"

"I . . . just . . ."

"Now!"

"Yes, ma'am." Then something caught Xander's eye. He let go of David and stepped into the tent.

"*Xander!*" David whispered harshly.

"Didn't you hear me?" the nurse said. "Two tents down!"

"Yes, ma'am," Xander repeated, but he continued into the tent. David saw that he was heading for a row of bodies lying near the side of the tent. A swath of tan canvas covered each body; only bare feet and hands protruded. On each covering was written a name: A. Powell, J. Davis . . . Xander bent and picked up the piece of charcoal beside the bodies.

"What are you doing?"

Yeah, David thought. *What are you doing!*

The nurse had reached the end of her patience with Xander. She screamed, "Help! Dr. Scott! Help!"

Xander darted to the tent flap and pushed David through it.

"What was that about?" David said. Then he realized that the nurse's yells were largely muffled by the tent material. With the yelling of commands to the soldiers and cries from the other wounded, no one would be able to hear her.

David pointed. "This way, I think. Dr. Scott, she said?"

"Hey," Xander scolded. "You're a prisoner."

They headed toward the tent she had indicated. Before reaching it, David felt a strong tug on his body, like a surf's undercurrent. Just as he realized what it was, Xander grabbed his shoulder.

"David!" he said. "The portal. My clothes are pulling me that way. The rifle too."

"I feel it too," David said. "Just go tell the doctor—"

"Are you crazy? We gotta go now. The portal moves. We can't risk losing it."

"But, Xander, that man."

"We're not supposed to be here," Xander said. "If he dies, that's the way it's supposed to be. Now, come on."

He grabbed David's collar again and yanked him toward where they both knew they would find the portal—beyond the row of tents opposite the ones Xander had been looking into.

David looked back at the tents. What if that man died because they didn't get the doctor for him? The nurse had not asked Xander for a glass of water but for a doctor, a lifesaver. He felt he was walking away from something important. The dying man was out of sight. And they weren't doctors. They couldn't *really* help the guy, could they? But did these things— that they couldn't see the person who needed help, that their help was limited to getting real help—mean they didn't have to try as hard as when David had saved the little girl from being run over by the Nazi tank?

Then again, Xander was right. They knew from watching the worlds through the doorways that the portals drifted around. It was as though they were caught in a river current. And they didn't know enough about how they worked to know for sure they wouldn't simply drift away or vanish altogether. If they didn't reach the portal when they had a chance, they could be stuck in Civil War world forever. They might die there—and sooner rather than later. What good would that do?

He let Xander pull him more easily toward the portal. Then his legs were moving fast alongside Xander's, and he pushed the dying man from his mind.

"Do you feel it?" he said. "Is the pull getting stronger? I can't tell."

"I think so. Come on." They ran between two tents. David thought he saw it: a hundred yards away where the field met the woods, the base of a tree seemed to shimmer and ripple, as though he were seeing it through the heat waves of fire.

"There it is!" David yelled and picked up his pace.

Xander grabbed his arm and stopped him. "Hold on a sec."

He ran back toward the front of the tent.

"Xander, come on! What are you doing?"

Xander disappeared around the edge of the tent. When David reached the corner, he found Xander drawing on the canvas of the tent with the charcoal he had picked up. David recognized the cartoon face that was his family's inside joke. The way he was drawing it, it would be four feet up, right on the front of the tent.

"What are you *doing?*" David yelled.

"I'll explain later," Xander said. "Go to the portal."

David looked back through the tents. His heart sank. The portal was gone. Then he saw it again, deeper into the woods. It was drifting. He knew at any moment it could just . . . float away.

"Hey, you!" someone yelled.

David turned to see a soldier standing in the camp's center aisle pointing at him—or at Xander, who was still drawing on the tent. Either way, this kind of attention wasn't good. Several of the pointing soldier's comrades turned to look. Whether they didn't like Xander defacing the tent or a Confederate soldier standing in their camp, unshackled and unguarded, he didn't know. But that something disturbed them was clear: two of the soldiers raised their rifles.

"Xander!" David yelled.

His brother's eyes darted toward him, then around to the object of David's concern. Xander dropped the chalk and bolted around the corner of the tent, slapping David on the back as he did. They ran for the woods.

Was the portal getting smaller or just farther away? Didn't matter—David would keep running until he reached it, and if he had to, he'd squeeze into a space the size of a mouse hole to get home.

Behind them someone yelled again, more insistently.

David's cast bounced against his ribs, causing jagged bolts of pain in both his arms and his ribs. The side of his jacket that had been hung loosely over his cast slipped off. It flapped behind him as he ran as fast as he could, staying right on Xander's heels.

A shot rang out. The musket ball tore through the woods ahead of them, sending branches and pine needles flipping through the air.

David would not have thought he could run any faster, but he did. He pulled even with Xander, then passed him.

Another shot, but he didn't see where that one went. A sickening thought crossed his mind. He yelled, "Xander?" He could not hear his brother's footsteps or breathing over his own.

He was ready to stop when Xander answered right behind him: "Go! Go!"

They hit the line of trees. David leaped over a tangle of branches. He came down on a small bush, almost fell, stayed up.

Without pausing, he ran directly into the shimmering, swirling portal.

CHAPTER

thirty-seven

TUESDAY, 1:22 A.M.

David was still running when he burst into the antechamber. He hit the far door at full speed. His cast hit first, then his knees and forehead. He began falling backward, when Xander came through the portal, just as fast. Xander slammed David back into the door. Both of them crashed to the floor.

"Ahhhg!" David screamed. It felt as though his entire left arm was on fire. The pain was so intense he saw nothing but a bright, blinding light in his head. He felt a hand clamp over his mouth.

"Shhh! You'll wake Dad."

"I . . . don't . . . care," David said through clenched teeth and Xander's hand. "My arm! My arm!"

Xander wrapped his arms around him, hugging him tightly, the way Dad would have done. "I know it hurts," he said, "but it's just your arm, Dae. You didn't get shot. You're alive."

It felt as though a sword had been run up the entire length of his arm. Slowly, while Xander rocked him, the agony diminished. The sword became a hot wire, then a throbbing pulse, like his blood was having a hard time traveling through the damaged highways of his veins and arteries.

After a while, David opened his eyes. They were sitting on the floor, leaning against the door he had crashed into. The portal door on the opposite side of the room was closed. Of course it was: it always slammed shut after a person went through. This time it had waited until both of them—Xander and David—had reentered the antechamber.

"Okay," David said, pushing Xander off him. "I'm okay." But he wasn't sure it was true. Each time his arm throbbed—which kept perfect time with the beating of his heart—pain shot into his shoulder and head. On the downbeats, when the pain took little breaks, his arm tingled. "My arm feels like it's asleep," he said. "When it's not—*uuuhhhgg*—killing me."

Xander scooted back on the floor and leaned into the bench. He was smiling.

"What's so funny?" David said. He was holding his teeth so tight against the pain, it felt like his molars would crumble.

"How many times did you get shot at?" Xander said. "And you wait till you get back home to get hurt."

"I got hurt *coming* home."

Xander shook his head, eyeing David. "You look terrible. Your face is covered with mud . . . where your tears didn't wash it away."

David touched his face. He had been in too much pain to even realize he had been crying about it. He kicked out at Xander's legs, striking him in the ankle.

"Hey," Xander said.

David said, "What was that, drawing Bob on the tent? We were almost free and clear until you stopped to do that."

Xander's expression grew solemn. "Something Dad thought of," he said. "It's a way of letting Mom know we were there. If she sees it, she'll know we're looking for her."

"But what if it doesn't last?" David said. "Does anything we do in those other worlds matter? Do they stay the way we left them?"

Xander thought for a minute. He looked at the portal door. "Maybe we should go back and see."

"No way!"

"I don't mean now. You know how the rooms change, how the things in the antechambers switch to something else?"

"Sometimes they're in another room. Sometimes they don't show up again until later."

"Same as the portals; the worlds are cycling through the house," Xander agreed. "There are twenty portals on this floor. What if there are a hundred different worlds? A thousand? It's like they move away from this house and then come back."

"Like a Ferris wheel," David suggested. "The seats move away from the guy who helps people get on at the bottom, then later on they come back down to him."

"Yeah, like that," Xander said. "But we don't know where the portals go when they move away from the house." He gestured toward the portal they had just stepped through. "Let's let it go away. When it comes back, we'll check it out, see if the world beyond is the way we just left it or if it reverts back to the way it was when we first found it."

David nodded, thinking. "So if it were a Ferris wheel and we left gum on the seat, would the gum be there when we saw the seat again, or would someone have cleaned it off?"

"Right," Xander said, smiling. "In this case, will Bob be there when we check again? It's exactly the kind of experiment Dad talked about."

David frowned. "How are we going to record what we learned if Dad doesn't even know we're doing this? You thought we could go over, take a quick look around, maybe find Mom. But, Xander . . ." He shook his head. "I don't think it's going to be that easy. Dad was right—we have to learn more about all of this. You can't take a quick look around when people are shooting at you."

"We're going to have to tell him, I guess," Xander said. He pointed a finger at David. "But he'd better get moving. I feel like we're dragging our feet."

David narrowed his eyes at his brother and said, "Don't talk about Dad like that. He's the one who thought up the control room. He's the one who knew it was going to take more than just popping in and out of the worlds to find Mom."

"Yeah, but we're the ones actually *doing* something."

That made David think of something his old soccer coach had said. "So we're the players and he's the coach," David suggested. "Together we're a team. We're in this together, right?"

"Together," Xander agreed. He smiled again at David. "You know how a hot shower feels so good after coming back from a world?"

"Like you're washing the bad stuff away," David said.

Xander gestured toward David's cast. "Let's wrap that in a trash bag. You *really* need a shower."

thirty-eight

TUESDAY, 8:50 A.M.

In school Tuesday morning, David could hardly keep his eyes open. He needed more sleep . . . and they needed to find Mom . . . and they needed to keep up the appearance of a normal life. How could they do it all? Dad always said things looked bleaker when you're tired. David didn't really believe a good night's sleep would give him a better attitude. But it sure would help him keep his eyes open.

His arm continued to throb. Every now and then it would send a searing hot dart into his shoulder, neck, and head. He wondered if it needed resetting or even if he'd broken it in another place. He didn't want to tell Dad about it, though. Dad would insist on taking David back to the doctor, which would give the doctor, and the *town*, more reason to believe that he was in danger—either from his own family or from the house. He would suffer through it and hope it got better.

"King?"

He heard Mrs. Moreau say his last name and realized she had been calling on him for some time. He raised his head, forcing his eyes to open wide. "Ma'am?"

She scowled at him with her birdlike features. "Are we asleep, Mr. King?"

He glanced around. All faces were turned toward him, smiling at his being caught unaware. "Uh . . ." he said. "*I'm* not."

"Then I must be boring you."

"No, ma'am."

Her narrow lips bent into a tight smile. "Would you come to the front, please?" she said.

David lowered his head, miserable. This was all he needed. He pushed himself out of his chair and walked to the front.

Mrs. Moreau said, "Please summarize today's lesson for the class."

There was a lesson?

Facing his classmates, he waited for something to come to him.

Surely *something* his teacher had said during the past hour had made it into his head. He could tell his class about meeting a Civil War general, about being shot at, and how it feels to run into a door with your broken arm. But he didn't think that's what she wanted from him. After a full minute of her letting him stand there looking stupid, he turned the most apologetic eyes he could muster on her.

"I'm sorry."

"Don't apologize to me, Mr. King," said Mrs. Moreau. "It's your classmates who suffer when you don't pay attention. Look at all the time you've wasted."

David scanned the faces staring back at him. A few nasty smiles, but mostly he saw sympathy. Probably they were just hoping they weren't next. He looked back at Mrs. Moreau, hoping to be excused to return to his chair. He saw only sly expectation on her face.

What does she want from me? he thought. Then he realized that she had been serious. In a low voice he asked her, "You want me to apologize to the class?"

"That would be nice."

He turned back to all the faces. "I'm sorry."

Mrs. Moreau touched his back as though they were buddies again. "Thank you, Mr. King. Don't let it happen again."

On the way back to his seat, his eyes landed on Clayton, the boy who had been sent to the principal's office for ridiculing David's name. Clayton gave him a stern look and ran his finger across his throat.

Oh, come on! David thought and sat down.

CHAPTER

thirty-nine

In his dream, the assassin was back home in Nineveh. He had just returned along with the Assyrian army from yet another conquest. Crowds filled the streets to cheer for the returning fighters and taunt the prisoners in their cages. Each of these cages was designed to hold a single person. They were small, even too small for children. But it was grown men and women who had been crammed into each of the hundreds of cages rolling into the city. Their howls of despair for their families, for themselves, rose above the cheers like the voices of a thousand souls condemned to Hades. Many would be removed from their cages and skinned alive during the coming days of celebration.

The assassin paced at the edge of the crowds, recognized but never acknowledged. No one dared to speak his name or even allow their eyes to dwell on him for more than a couple of seconds. He knew that their collective voices thanked him for his role in the conquest. That knowledge and their fear were gratitude enough.

As he watched, a soldier drew his sword and held it high. The man pointed to the fingers of a prisoner, which were protruding from the iron bars of his cage. The crowd roared louder. The soldier brought down his sword, skimming it along the bars. Sparks flew up and the fingers came off. The soldier leaned over and used the tip of his sword to flick the fingers into the crowd. The citizens of the assassin's capital city scrambled for these treasures. They would be added to the ever-changing, ever-decaying "works of art" the citizens kept in their homes, art made exclusively of the body parts of their conquered enemies. It was their way of honoring the gods for their victories and their expanding empire. It reminded every Assyrian both of their power and the fragility of their mortal bodies. They had to stay strong, had to keep conquering, or they themselves would end up as artwork in another man's home.

Striding past a cart of caged prisoners, the assassin paused. The crowd was pointing to something just beyond him, urging him to act. Toes protruded from a cage. In one swift motion the assassin unsheathed his sword and brought it down on the toes. The woman inside the cage bellowed in pain and turned her face to the assassin.

He reeled back as he recognized his own mother.

Taksidian bolted straight up in his hotel bed, gasping for

breath. Sweat coated his body and drenched his sheets. They clung to him like a specter, trying to pull him back into the nightmare. He peeled them off his body and tossed them to the floor. He ran his fingers up his face, catching the strands of hair that were plastered there and pushing them back over his head. He leaned his head back and moaned.

Would the nightmare never leave him alone? For more than thirty years it had haunted him. Despite the wealth he had amassed, the luxuries to which he had grown accustomed, ever since he had stepped from the world of his birth into that house, his sleeping mind never let him forget. The world from which he came was violent and bloody, and indeed his mother, his whole family, had been slaughtered. But he had not taken part, except to know what happened as part of the process to harden his heart and prepare him for the life of an assassin.

He rose from his bed and stretched, feeling his joints pop, his muscles flex. Age was catching up to him, and he still had so much more to do. He strode to the curtains and parted them. Daylight streamed in, stinging his eyes. What little sleep he allowed himself he always got during the day. Night was too valuable to waste on sleep. It was for working without interruption. And for stealth.

He went into the bathroom and turned on the shower. While the water heated, he leaned against the countertop to stare at his reflection in the mirror. His face was still lean, his eyes bright. Had he remained in Assyria, had he gone back, he would have certainly been dead by now. No Assyrian lived past the age of forty, and the assassin who saw his thirtieth birthday was rare. Here he was, almost sixty and still kicking. Kicking hard.

He glanced at his watch. 1:13. Good. Still time to get to the house before that family returned from school. He had news to gather and instructions to give. He bristled at the thought of the King family. They were a thorn in his side.

No matter, he thought as he turned back to the running water and checked its temperature. Soon enough, he would pluck them from his flesh and flick them away—like fingers under the tip of a sword.

CHAPTER

TUESDAY, 3:00 P.M.

Throughout that second day of school, David kept an eye on
Clayton. He watched him in the hallways between classes and
at lunch. When he saw David looking, the boy merely smiled.
It was not until the final bell rang that Clayton made his move.
As David was leaving his last class, Clayton slipped into the
room. He grabbed David's cast, sending a fresh bolt of pain
into David's shoulder.

"Let's talk," Clayton said.

"I don't think so," David said. He tried to shake his arm free, but Clayton had a good grip, and pain kept David's movements to a minimum. "Let go," David said, trying to look fierce.

Another boy, taller than either of them, stepped up beside Clayton. David knew his name was Joe.

He jerked his head to indicate the classroom behind David. "Get in there, King," he said quietly.

Other kids streamed past them and glanced back knowingly.

David took a step back. Clayton and Joe stayed right on him.

Clayton turned to the teacher, who was erasing the white marker board at the front of the classroom. He used his sweetest voice to say, "Mrs. Hammerstrom, Mr. Reid is look-ing for you."

"Oh," Mrs. Hammerstrom said, setting the eraser down and smoothing the wrinkles out of her blouse and skirt. She hurried out of the room, her heels *clack-clack-clacking*.

The sound was harsh in David's ears, which struck him as sadly appropriate for the situation he was in.

"Let's sit," Clayton told him.

"You don't want to sit," David said.

"I do, for a while," Clayton said, smiling. "At least until the school clears out a bit. We don't want your screams to draw too much attention."

"Clayton, it's not my fault you went to the office."

"Oh, really? Whose fault is it, then? Let's see, it was your stupid name that got me in trouble, and it was your stupid father I had to go see."

David stuck out his chest and bumped Clayton with it. "He's not stupid."

Clayton was taller than David by at least two inches. When he bumped back, David had to take a step to keep from falling.

"Stupid enough," Clayton said and laughed, as though he had said something clever.

"Look, you want to fight. I get it. But how tough are you, beating up on a kid with a broken arm? Wait until I get this cast off, and we'll make it fair."

Clayton's palm slammed into David's chest. David stumbled into a desk and fell backward hard. The desk fell with him, and the seat back cracked him on the head. He rubbed the spot, already feeling a knot starting to swell under his hair. He looked up at Clayton's and Joe's grinning faces and said, "Mrs. Hammerstrom will be coming back."

"Not for a while," Clayton said, laughing. "I saw Mr. Reid take off in his car after last period. He's the assisstant principal, you know. Her boss. She'll look everywhere before giving up." He slapped Joe in the arm with the back of his hand. "Shut the door."

David watched Joe lean into the hallway, look in both directions, then shut the door.

"Clearing out fast," Joe reported.

Clayton's grin grew wider.

"My dad's waiting for me," David said. "We pick up my sister right after school."

"He'll wait for you," Clayton said.

"Or he *won't*," Joe added and laughed.

"Either way, this won't take long," Clayton said.

David really didn't need this. He was tired. He was hurt. He just wanted to go home and find his mother. He said, "My father will send in my brother to look for me." He tried to make it sound like a fact, not a threat.

"*Oooh*, your brother. I'm scared. Joe, you scared?"

"Shaking in my boots," Joe said. He laughed again.

Clayton hardened his face into a mask of meanness. He said, "We'll just have to kick both your butts. Two Kings for the price of one."

David didn't like Clayton thinking he could own Xander. "He's fifteen, my brother. A lot bigger than you."

"I know who he is," Clayton sneered. "You don't think you can just move here without everyone knowing everything about you, do you?"

Not everything, David thought. *If you did, your little mind would explode.* He wanted to say it, but settled for saying, "You don't know *anything*."

"I know you moved into the old haunted house outside of town," he said.

David felt sick. "It's not haunted," he said.

"Everyone knows it is," Clayton said. "Right, Joe?"

Joe nodded.

"Last family that lived there, the father killed 'em all, then killed himself."

"Did not," David said. He warned himself to shut up, just shut up.

"Did too. Maybe your daddy's going to do the same to you too. Is that how you broke your arm? Daddy try to kill you?"

David lowered his head. Not seeing Clayton's sour face helped David bite his tongue.

"Yeah, that's what I heard. Your daddy broke your arm. That's what everyone's saying. Huh, Joe?"

"Twisted it until it just snapped like a twig," Joe confirmed. "Heard you cried like a girl."

Stay down, David told himself. *He wants me to fight. Then he could say I started it.*

Clayton said, "The whole town is so convinced your dad's banging you around, I can pound you to a pulp and no one'll believe that I did it."

"I fell out of a tree," David said quietly.

Clayton laughed. "Oh, is that the best you and your old man could come up with? Fell out of a tree?" He stepped closer, reached down, and grabbed a fistful of David's shirt.

David swung his good arm up, knocking Clayton's hand away.

Clayton looked surprised by David's boldness. He said, "That'll cost you another broken arm, dude." He circled around to David's left side, obviously looking for an easier angle of attack.

Outside, a car horn honked. Joe looked through the windows at the back of the room. "Clay, I think it's his old man."

Clayton crouched. "Get down! Get down! Did he see you?"

"I don't think so. He's out in the parking lot . . ."

The horn sounded again.

"Honking," Joe said.

"No kidding? Go look."

Joe waddled in a crouch to the windows. He peered over the sill. "He's just sitting—"

David lurched forward. Clayton grabbed for him. David swung his arm and smashed his cast into Clayton's mouth. The boy yelled and flew backward. David pushed himself up and darted for the door. Clayton was wailing behind him.

David didn't look back. He pulled open the door and ran into the hallway. He turned right, toward the main entrance, and beat his feet against the tile floor, wanting only to put distance between himself and Clayton. He realized too late that he'd made a mistake. He was heading toward the cafeteria, not the front entrance. He stopped to turn around and saw Clayton and Joe emerge from the classroom. Blood coated Clayton's lip and chin.

The boy saw him, spat on the floor, and smiled. He started toward David.

David ran for the cafeteria door and hit the bar that opened it. He would have been better off slamming into a brick wall.

He banged his cast on the door—*again!*—and bounced off. The doors were locked.

Man, they shut down early around here, he thought.

He scrambled to his feet. Clayton and Joe were ambling slowly toward him, knowing he was cornered, savoring his fear. The only other exit David knew about was on the far end of the hallway, past the boys who wanted to pound him to a pulp. He was near the short leg of hallway that had been his introduction to the building's interior—the first he had seen of the school when he had portaled from the linen closet to the locker.

The locker, number 119. It was right there, not fifty feet away. He could probably reach it before Clayton and Joe got to where they could see him go into it. Did he dare?

He thought about Clayton—madder than ever, bloody lip and all.

It wasn't a difficult decision.

He darted into the short hallway, directly toward the center locker, the locker that was the way out of this mess.

From around the corner, Clayton called, "That's a dead end, King David! You're stupid, just like your dad."

As he approached the locker, David's eyes focused on the latch. *Please, please, please*, he thought. *Don't be locked.* He saw that there was no lock on it yet, and his heart was thankful for the break. His sneakers squeaked to a stop in front of it. He had the latch lifted and the door opened before the momentum of his body had slowed. It was empty.

"Ollie, ollie oxen free," Clayton called.

Quickly he looked in their direction. They hadn't come around the corner yet. David climbed in and pulled the door closed behind him.

CHAPTER

forty-one

TUESDAY, 3:21 P.M.

David felt the sides of the locker move away from his shoulders. Instead of metal and pencil shavings, he smelled wood and fresh laundry. Instead of a thin steel floor under his feet, which buckled a little when he shifted his weight, he was standing on solid floorboards. Even the quality of the darkness had changed, reflecting the difference between the light that came through the locker vents and the dimmer illumination of his home's upstairs hallway as it seeped through the crack under the door. He opened the door and stepped into the hallway, pulling in a deep breath. As he released it, he released the tension of knowing he was about to get pounded. He smiled at the thought of Clayton and Joe coming around the corner and not finding him.

The possibility of their having witnessed his vanishing inside locker 119 brought a tinge of concern back to his stomach. But compared to the beating Clayton had promised, it was a concern he could live with. He would not be able to avoid Clayton forever, but at least this gave him time to figure out what to do about the school bully.

He shut the linen closet door and glanced around. Home. He had never been there alone before. It was a little creepy, the silence, the stillness. The only light came from the sun, filtered through the trees outside and the bedroom windows. It gave the house an unlived-in, museumlike feel.

He bit his bottom lip. Dad was waiting for him at school—honking for him to come out. He did not know about the portal from school to home. After Mom had been taken and Dad had come clean about having lived in the house before and knowing its secrets—though apparently not *this* one—he and Xander should have told him about the linen closet. David wasn't sure why they hadn't, except that it seemed everything had been moving a thousand miles a minute since Mom's kidnapping. They just hadn't had time.

He felt a pang of guilt, knowing there were other reasons as well: David and Xander *liked* knowing something about the house Dad didn't, and what if they wanted to *use* the portal sometime? They didn't want Dad restricting them or jumping all over them. And that they had kept it a secret this long would make telling Dad about it that much harder.

There was no way Xander would say anything, no way he would even suspect that David had used the portal now. He and Dad would just keep waiting for him. When he didn't come out, they would probably search the school. All the while, Toria would be waiting at her elementary school. Dad would be worried sick.

David would have to go back through and meet Dad at the school. Of course, he'd need to wait until he was sure Clayton and Joe had given up looking for him. That would give him time to think of an excuse for being late.

A murmuring reached his ears. It had the rhythm and alternating tones of human conversation. He wondered if someone had left a radio on. Dad liked to listen to what he called "talking heads" in the mornings.

David crept down the hall to the banister that overlooked the foyer. He leaned over the railing but could no longer hear the voices. Something creaked, and he realized it was overhead—from the third-floor hallway. His heart began to race as he thought of the big, bare footprints they had found in the house and the man who had taken Mom. Had he returned? Or was it someone else?

He detected the murmuring again: a deep rumbling of spoken

words, followed by more words in a slightly higher tone. *Two people!*

The footprints they had found had all been similar. They had assumed that someone—as in *one* person—had been in the house. But David was hearing *two* voices! He crept farther down the hall past the master bedroom door on his left. For just a moment he was terribly sure that he had misjudged where the creak and the voices had come from. After all, how could you tell in a house that played with sounds the way children played with marbles?

He was frozen in front of the master bedroom's open door, sure that if he turned to look, two people would be looking back at him. Then a man said something in a sharp tone. It was not as near as the bedroom, and David felt relief. He turned his head and saw no one in the room. He continued to the end of the hallway. Here, a second hallway branched toward the back of the house. The secret panel at the end was hinged open. He tiptoed toward it. The door to what was now the MCC came up on the right. But the voices were clearer now—and definitely coming from upstairs.

David reached the secret panel and leaned through the opening.

A rumbling voice drifted to him from the upstairs hallway. He furrowed his brow in concentration. He did not understand the words he was hearing.

As though reading his thoughts, a different voice said, "In

English. If I ever need your help outside this house, in this time, you will need to speak the language of the day."

As deep as this English-speaking voice was, the other man's was deeper. It rumbled like boulders in an avalanche, but much slower. It said, "Not . . . easy."

"I know. We'll work on it. I have another mission for you."

David heard the rustling of paper.

"This man . . . see, here? Must not reach his destination."

The boulder-voice said, "Want . . . kill?"

"Of course. Do what you do best."

Boulder-man grunted.

"You'll find him here . . . in this world. Look for the—"

Trying to hear, David stepped through the secret panel. His cast thunked against the door. He froze in place and held his breath. Silence. The men upstairs had stopped talking. Then came the sudden sound of footsteps—two sets of them, moving fast, growing louder.

David spun around, already moving out of the hidden panel's threshold. His cast hit the door again, louder this time. He didn't care. He shoved his shoulder into it. It flew open and crashed into the hallway wall. He was at the junction of the upstairs hallways when he heard a clattering of shoes on the stairs behind him. A more muffled pounding made him think of the barefoot giant who had taken Mom. A man with shoes, a man without: David had no desire to meet either one.

He moved as fast as he could, past the master bedroom, the

landing, Toria's room, the bathroom. Three doors lay ahead: his and Xander's room, the spare bedroom, and the linen closet. He had to reach the linen closet before his pursuers rounded the corner. He gritted his teeth and willed his feet to move faster. He reached the closet door, opened it, and stopped.

At the far end of the hallway, Taksidian came racing around the corner. He saw David and paused. The only sounds were David's panicked breathing and the footsteps of the barefoot man hurrying to catch up.

Taksidian said, "*Boy!*"

David scrambled into the closet and slammed the door. He felt the air change around him, the walls press in.

Come on, come on! he thought.

When light appeared before him, forming itself into the vents of the locker door, he pushed it open to step through.

It was only at this moment that he even considered the possibility of Clayton still looking for him in the short hallway.

Who cares? he thought. *Clayton or Taksidian? No contest.*

Still, it would be a disaster if Clayton found out about—

Hands grabbed his shirt and yanked him out of the locker.

CHAPTER

forty-two

"What are you doing?" Xander said. Gripping David's shirt, he gave him a shake. "What were you doing in there?"

David looked back at the open locker and said, "Taksidian's right behind me. He saw me go into the closet."

Xander's jaw tightened. "What? Why did you go through?"

"Clayton—"

"Never mind!" Xander said. He shoved David aside and reached for the locker door.

"Wait!" David said. "Does it work if the door's left open? What if he can't follow me here if we don't shut it?"

Xander flashed an expression at David that was part confusion, part frustration. He backed away from the locker. "And what if he just appears in the locker?" He snapped his fingers. "Okay, okay, I have an idea. Wait here." He ran out of the short hallway and around the corner.

"Xander!" David yelled. "Xander!"

"Wait there a sec!" He sounded pretty far away. "If Taksidian shows up—*run!*"

David backed away from the locker. He kept his eyes on its dark interior. Did something move in there? He squinted. Nah, just shadows. He heard footsteps, and his stomach cramped. Could sounds come through before a person did?

Then Xander came jogging around the corner. Reaching the locker, he said, "Okay," and slammed the door closed.

"Xander, no!" David said.

"I got it, I got it." Xander slipped a combination lock through the hole in the latch. He smiled at David. "See?"

Bang!

Something slammed against the locker door from the other side.

Xander jumped, and David screamed.

Bang! Bang! Bang!

David started to run, but Xander grabbed his arm to stop him. Xander whispered, "It's locked. He can't get through."

"He could break the lock," David said.

Bang! Bang! Bang!

Xander pressed his lips together. He stepped close to the locker and held his hand up to it, but didn't actually touch it. He said, "Leave us alone."

The banging stopped. Xander looked at David. David shrugged.

A voice came through the door. It was deep and echoey from the smooth metal walls inside. "Leave the house, and I'll let you be."

The words chilled David's skin. He stepped forward and said, "We want our mother back."

Silence. Then: "I don't have her."

David said, "Did you take her?"

More silence . . . longer. David was about to repeat his question when Taksidian said, "You should know by now, nothing about that house is as simple as that."

Xander slammed his fist against the locker door. "Did you take her or not?"

They waited for a reply. And waited.

David yelled, "Do you know about our mother?"

After a minute of silence, Xander whispered, "I don't think he's in there."

"How could he leave? I thought you had to open and shut the door?"

Xander shook his head. "Maybe he just made his point: nothing is as simple as that."

David said, "Want to look?"

"No way."

David stepped past him and pressed his ear against the door. He squeezed his eyes shut in anticipation of a *bang!* suddenly breaking his eardrum. He heard nothing inside. No breathing, no metal buckling under shifted weight. He squinted up into the vents. Only blackness.

"If he's not in there, he's in our house," Xander said.

"With the big barefoot guy," David agreed. To Xander's puzzled expression, he said, "I'll tell you later. Dad needs to hear it too."

Xander nodded toward the locker. He said, "Is there stuff in there? Books, a jacket, like someone's using it?"

"I didn't see anything."

Xander stepped closer. He licked his lips, then began slowly turning the dial on the combination lock.

"What are you doing?" David hissed.

"We don't know if this locker has been assigned or not. Either way, a lock will draw attention to it. And we had to give them our combinations, in case they want to open them and not use bolt cutters. I don't want any school officials even *thinking* about this locker. And I definitely don't want them thinking about *me* and this locker."

"Like someone's going to take the time to test every combination they have to see whose lock it is," David said.

"If they figure out the locker does weird things, they will," Xander said, leaning closer to the dial. The lock snapped open.

Before he could slip it off the latch, David grabbed Xander's fingers and the lock. He whispered, "What if he's in there?"

"Get ready to run."

With the care and slowness of a demolition expert snipping the wires of a bomb, Xander maneuvered the lock out of the hole in the latch. As soon as it was clear, he backpedaled away. David matched his steps, never taking his eyes off the locker door.

They waited. Finally, Xander nudged him. He gestured with his head and started for the bend in the hallway. They went around it and headed toward the double doors at the far end, snapping their eyes over their shoulders to make sure no one was following.

When it seemed safe to talk again, Xander said, "There were two kids roaming around when I came in looking for you. Are they part of this?"

David said, "I was trying to hide from them."

"In the locker?"

David nodded.

"And you ran into Taksidian? Your luck just seems to get better and better, doesn't it?"

"Tell me about it," David said.

· · · · · · · ·

By the time they reached home, David had told his father about the linen closet portal, his passage through it that afternoon, and his encounter with Taksidian. Xander confessed his role in keeping the linen closet secret and helped David explain the part about talking to Taksidian through the locker door.

Dad stopped the SUV at the end of the street in front of their house. He sat there with the engine idling, peering through the windshield. Xander turned in the front seat to exchange a worried look with David. Even Toria understood the significance of it all and remained quiet.

"Well," Dad said finally. "I can't say I'm happy about your keeping the closet a secret, but I understand." He reached out and gripped Xander's shoulder. "And I suppose I don't have the best track record for honesty myself right now. But no more secrets, okay?"

Xander nodded.

Dad threw his arm over the back of the seat and gazed at David. "Okay?"

"Um . . . Dad?" David said, wondering how his father was going to take the news of his sons getting shot at on some Civil War battlefield. "Last night—"

"I woke him up again," Xander interrupted. He gave David a quick scowl—there and gone. "We . . . looked for that guy again who was watching the house." He smiled, a little too broadly. "We didn't see anybody."

Dad looked from Xander to David, back to Xander.

He knows something's up, David thought, miserable.

But instead of quizzing them, Dad simply nodded.

David leaned forward and turned his head to peer at the house. "What if they're still in there?"

"Daddy?" Toria said, sounding frightened.

Dad looked through the window at the house. "Okay. We'll search the house together."

"With knives?" Xander suggested.

"No!" Dad said, pointing at his oldest son. "We'll just . . . grab something to defend ourselves when we get in there. No knives." He killed the engine, and they all got out.

As Dad unlocked the front door, David edged close to him.

"Dad?" He touched his father's arm. When he got no answer he said, more insistently, "Dad!" and gave him a push.

"What, Dae?"

Instead of answering, he pointed. Thirty or forty feet beyond the side of the house, a man stood in the woods. He wore a dark overcoat like Taksidian's, but it wasn't Taksidian.

"What the—?" Dad said. Without taking his eyes off the stranger, he descended the porch steps.

"Dad . . ." Xander said.

"I'm taking care of it, Xander," his Dad replied.

Xander said, "No, Dad, look."

Dad looked up at Xander; then his eyes followed Xander's pointing finger toward the opposite side of the house. There, deep in the woods, stood another man. Dad looked again at the first stranger and took a step toward him. He called out, "You're on private property! I'm calling the police." He went to the door and pushed it open. "Come on, kids."

"Who are those men, Daddy?" Toria asked.

"Just people trying to scare us."

"Why?"

"I don't know, sweetie. Xander, shut the door. Make sure it's locked. Let's take a look around."

"Are you gonna call the cops?" David asked.

Dad frowned at him. "Probably not. I'm not sure anyone in this town is on our side."

CHAPTER

forty-three

They searched the house and found nothing. Even the secret door in the wall was shut and looking just as it should. David was glad that Xander had heard Taksidian pound on the locker door. Otherwise, he would have wondered if his family really believed everything he had said about that afternoon. After the search, Dad and Toria went to the kitchen to start dinner. David and Xander found themselves in the MCC.

"Why didn't you let me tell Dad about last night, about going through the portal to the Civil War?" David said in a harsh whisper.

Xander squatted by the rolls of movie posters. He picked up one and unrolled it just enough to see what movie it advertised. "If we tell him now, he won't let us go back into it."

"What? To that same world? Why would we want to?"

Xander raised his eyebrows at him. "Because we're trying to find Mom, remember?"

"Dad knows that," David said. "He's not against us going over. He just wants to do it safely."

Xander dropped the poster and picked up another one. "And what does that mean, exactly? I don't even think Dad knows. Why isn't he up here now, planning a trip through a portal to find Mom, instead of downstairs making dinner?"

"Xander, I almost got killed last night—again! I thought we agreed we can't just hop into these worlds, grab Mom, and bring her back. Not unless she happens to be strolling around right where we appear, and that doesn't seem very likely. And it's like everywhere we go, someone's trying to kill us. Xander, listen to me!" He waited for his brother to look at him. "I'm totally with you—but we need Dad too. We need to do this smart." David's shoulders dropped, and he couldn't help feeling a little sorry for himself and a lot sorry for Mom.

Xander dropped the poster and stood. "All right, but let's

do one thing that will show Dad we aren't just being . . . *rebellious*. Let's show him that our hearts are in the right place."

"How?"

"He's the one who suggested putting something in each world that Mom would recognize so she'll know we're looking for her."

"Bob," David said.

Xander nodded. "But Dad didn't know if it would stay there after we left. We don't want to be going through all these worlds, taking the time to leave a message for her in each one just to have it disappear from that world when we come back to the house. If we can just give Dad something solid, a positive yes-it's-still-there or no-it's-not . . . ." He shrugged. "Then at least he'd know."

"A rule," David said. "Dad likes to know the rules. But how are we going to—"

"We go back and look. Right now. All we have to do is go in, see if Bob is still on the tent, and get out."

David glared at his brother. His stomach and throat were so tight he wasn't sure he could speak, but he did: "Xander, I *can't*. The bullets were like . . . I mean, I heard them zipping past my head. I . . ."

"Okay, okay," Xander said. "Then, just come up with me. Help me find the room and wait for me. In case I need you."

"Don't go."

"I have to, Dae." He stepped over the posters to grip David's good arm. "Look around. This room is *all* we've done to find Mom." He shook his head, obviously frustrated. "You stepped into that World War II village, but that was almost an accident. We're supposed to be *doing* something."

David bit his lip. "We promised: no more secrets. Dad's told us how many times, Xander? The portals are off-limits . . . at least when he's not with us. It's only been two days since Mom was taken. Give Dad some time—"

"We don't *have* time!" Xander said forcefully, but not with enough volume to warn Dad of their argument. "*Mom* doesn't have time." He closed his eyes, then opened them slowly. "Let's do this one thing."

"When does the sneaking stop?" David asked. "First Dad didn't tell us the real reason we moved here. Then we started sneaking through portals into other worlds, even after Dad told us not to. When does it stop, Xander?"

Xander held up his index finger. He said, "After this one thing. Dad would say, 'No, it's too dangerous. We don't know enough yet.' But maybe if he saw progress—you know, if we showed him that the way to learn things, to get closer to finding Mom, is to go over and not just talk about it—then maybe he'd get going and *do* something."

David just frowned.

Xander continued: "When you wanted to see for yourself what those doors were all about, when you thought Dad was going to take us away, you said you'd go over with or without me."

David's eyes narrowed. "So?"

"So, I'm going to do this whether you help or not."

"That's not fair. That was before Mom—"

"Are you in or out, Dae? That's all I need to know."

Xander was probably right that Dad would nix this plan in a heartbeat. It was also likely that handing Dad proof that they were learning about the other worlds would psych him up to take more action.

But they had *promised*. How many more broken promises would it take for Dad to completely lose his trust in them? Then he would definitely take them away, because he wouldn't be able to trust them to be safe.

In the end, it was the determination in Xander's face that made up David's mind. He said, "I'll help you this one last time. But I mean it, Xander. No more secrets. We do this as a family . . . or not at all."

Xander smiled. "Agreed." He stood there, waiting for something.

"What?" David said.

"I need to hear you say it, man. Come on, for me."

David gave him a lopsided grin. He said, "Let's do it."

•••••••••

David and Xander each took one side of the hallway. They moved from door to door, checking each antechamber for the Civil War items they had worn the night before.

"Dae," Xander said. He was clearly thinking something through. "If you see the items from when Dad and I went over—you know, the picnic stuff—let me know. We can find out what we need there too."

"Bob?" David asked.

"Yeah. Remember I said Dad carved him into a tree?"

David opened a door and saw a well-used painter's smock, a rosary, a wooden mallet, and some other things that were definitely not related to the Civil War. He closed the door and moved on to the next one. When he reached the end of the crooked hall, he started back, looking into the rooms he had seen just minutes before. It gave him an uneasy feeling to find that the items inside each one had already changed. Where the smock, rosary, and mallet had been were now a bridle, reins, and riding crop.

On the third lap through the doors, David said, "Dad's going to wonder where we are."

Xander opened and closed a door, then headed for the next one. "He's got spaghetti with meat sauce cooking. I can smell it. That always takes forever. Besides, when dinner's ready, he'll probably send Toria—" He opened a door and stopped, then smiled at David. "Bingo."

CHAPTER

forty-four

MIDWAY INTERNATIONAL AIRPORT, CHICAGO

Keal looked like he was going to be sick. His face glistened with sweat. His eyes kept darting one direction, then another.

Jesse stretched out his fingers and patted the back of Keal's hand. The big black man actually jumped in his chair.

Jesse smiled. "It's okay."

"Okay?" Keal whispered. He lowered his head, even though they were the only people in the waiting area of Gate A19.

"I've *kidnapped* you, man." He snapped his head up and shot glances all around.

"It's not kidnapping if I asked you to take me."

"You don't understand," Keal said. "You're an old man in a nursing home where I work. They'll say I took you against your will or that I took advantage of your senility to talk you into coming with me."

"I'm not senile."

"You're *old*," Keal said, making the word sound like a disease. He tapped his temple. "They'll say you've lost it, even if you haven't."

Jesse shook his head. "Why would you want to kidnap me?"

Keal started to say something, then stopped. His eyes snapped to a police officer strolling casually along the concourse. He waggled a finger at Jesse, and his deep voice grew even quieter. "All I'm saying is you better be right."

Jesse pulled in a long breath. He frowned and scrunched his brows together, then said, "You're doing the right thing, Keal. I appreciate it."

"I mean," Keal said, "I don't want anyone to be in danger, but when we get there, there better be people to save, you know?"

"There will be," Jesse said. He got hold of Keal's big hand again and squeezed. "You wouldn't believe how many people you're saving by taking me home."

He leaned back in his wheelchair. A sign behind the empty

counter confirmed that the gate serviced a flight that would take them to Redding, California—a ninety-minute drive from Pinedale. It was scheduled to leave in just under two hours.

Jesse caught Keal looking at him with unsure eyes, and he smiled again. He whispered, "Thank you," then lowered his eyelids to catch a few winks before takeoff.

CHAPTER

forty-five

TUESDAY, 6:50 P.M.

David paced the little room. From the portal to the open hallway door, he could take only five good steps. No wonder he had crashed so painfully into the door the night before. The other direction, from the bench to the wall, was only three steps. He supposed it was all the space that was required: pick up a map, throw on some clothes, maybe change your shoes. What more did you need to venture into a different world? He looked at the gray coat hanging from a hook. It was still dirty from when he had hit the ground, trying to keep a musket ball from taking off his head. Perhaps he should have gone over with Xander again, but every time he thought of those soldiers firing at him, he felt sick.

Just come back, Xander. Please.

David didn't wear a watch, but he felt his brother had been gone fifteen minutes or so. If he had stepped onto the same battlefield they had the night before, he should be able to reach the tents and find the portal home in about five more minutes.

He heard footsteps pounding toward him, and he froze. Someone was hurrying up the stairs.

Toria's voice reached him: "Xander! David! Are you up here?" Her voice was shrill with panic, and he realized she wasn't calling them for dinner.

He stepped into the hallway. "Here!" David said. "What is it?"

Toria bounded into the hallway and stopped. Her eyes were wide. "Cops!" she said, out of breath. "They're at the door. Dad's arguing with them. They want us to leave."

David looked back into the antechamber at the closed portal door. Could he just leave Xander? Would it be okay? He thought about propping open the hallway door—maybe that would keep anything from happening up here while he ran down to find out what was going on. But if he'd learned anything about the house, it was that it would do what it wanted to do. It didn't matter if they propped open a door or locked it or whatever. Maybe by the time David got downstairs, Dad would have taken care of the situation, and David could be back before Xander returned.

He strode toward Toria. "What's Dad doing?"

"Nothing, just saying they don't have the right to make us leave."

David darted around her and raced down the hidden staircase. Hearing angry voices, he paused at the secret doorway in the upstairs hall.

"I don't care what that piece of paper says," Dad said. "You can't just—"

"Sir, where are the children?"

"That's my business. Hey! Hey! I said no, you can't come in!"

Toria stepped up behind David. She whispered, "Where's Xander?"

"Shhh." He walked past the MCC and turned into the second floor's main hallway. The voices were booming up from the foyer. Stopping at the top of the stairs, he couldn't believe what was happening in the entryway below.

The door was open, and two uniformed police officers were grabbing at Dad. One seized his arm and twisted it, forcing him to spin around. They pushed him face-first into the wall. David saw a flash of bright metal and realized they were about to slap handcuffs on his father.

"Daddy!" Toria screamed and ran past David. He tried to

stop her, but she slipped out of his grasp and started down the stairs.

The handcuffs clicked, binding Dad's wrists behind his back. One of the cops pushed his hand into Dad's back, keeping Dad's cheek pressed against the wall as though it were glued there. Dad strained to get a look at Toria coming down the stairs.

"Stay there, honey!" Dad yelled.

"Come here, sweetheart," the other cop said, gesturing with his hand.

Toria braked before reaching the foyer. "Daddy?"

Dad's eyes rolled and found David. "David, where's Xander?"

"He's . . . uh . . ."

"Go get him!"

"But . . ."

The cop who'd spoken to Toria was looking at David now. He said, "Come down here, son."

"No!" Dad yelled. "David, go get your brother."

A movement in the open doorway caught David's attention. Taksidian stepped into view and leaned casually against the frame. He took in the scene, then his eyes flicked up to David. The man smiled thinly.

Dad caught sight of him. He said, "Is *he* why you're doing this? That man wants my house!"

The cop holding him spun him around. "We don't know about that, sir. We're just doing our jobs."

The other cop beckoned to David again. "Son, you'll have to come with us."

David backed away from the stairs. He was about to turn and run when he heard a sound. It was the *click!* of a door handle's latch. It had come from down the hall, toward Xander and David's bedroom.

Toward the linen closet!

Just as the thought came to him, the closet door swung open. Already beating impossibly fast, his heart went into overdrive.

Clayton stepped out of the closet and looked around, wide-eyed and openmouthed. He looked as though he thought he was dreaming. He squinted at David, and said, "King David?"

David was sure his own expression was just as stunned.

"Who's that?" asked one of the cops below—from the foyer, the closet was out of sight.

The other answered, "Must be the older boy. Both of you, come on down!"

David glanced over the banister at the men, their faces turned up, growing impatient. Realizing something was up, Taksidian's smile faded. He scowled at David.

Without a word, David headed toward Clayton. If he simply left him there, eventually the kid would find the cops or the cops would find him—then he'd start talking: *I stepped into a locker at school and wound up here! No, really!* David wasn't sure exactly what he could do to prevent that, but he had to do *something*. Should he take Clayton with him to get Xander?

What if he didn't want to come? The boy was bigger than David; it wasn't like David could just *drag* him—especially past the cops. Even if he could take him, that would mean showing Clayton the third floor. It was enough he'd found the locker-to-closet portal; did they really want him knowing everything?

The bully was standing in the closet doorway, his fingers on the handle. As David approached, Clayton's face twisted into a nasty smirk. "What kind of freak-thing you got going on here, twerp?"

David put his palm on Clayton's chest and shoved him back into the closet.

Clayton's eyes flashed wide as he fell back. "Hey—!"

David slammed the door shut. He heard a whoosh of air from the gap under the door: Clayton was heading back to the locker. David went into his bedroom, grabbed a chair, and dragged it into the hall. He wedged the seat back under the closet's door handle. He leaned close to listen. No sound from inside. It wouldn't take long for Clayton to figure out that he could return to the house by opening and closing the locker door. Then what? He'd start pounding.

At least this bought David some time. Maybe Clayton would be too freaked-out to come back. Maybe the cops would leave before he returned. Maybe Xander would have a plan.

Too many maybes!

David ran down the hall, intent on finding his brother. As

he passed the foyer, a cop yelled up: "Hey, kid! Stop! Hold it right there!"

David rounded the corner and shot through the passageway where the fake wall was hinged open. He turned and pulled it closed, tugging until he heard it click. Then he bolted up the stairs. Xander wasn't in the antechamber when he got there. Panting, David stared at the door, willing it to open, willing his brother to step through. Gritting his teeth, thinking of nothing else to do, he yanked the gray jacket off the hook and slipped it on.

Maybe I can take it off when I get there, he thought. *Roll it up under my shirt before they start shooting at me.*

His stomach lurched. His guts tightened in fear, and he had to close his eyes until the feeling passed.

Got to find Xander. As soon as I get there, I'll just run, run straight for the camp.

He reached up for the dirty gray kepi.

The portal door burst open. Blinding sunlight. A gust of wind blew in. Smoke stung his nostrils. Grains of dirt peppered his cheeks.

The door slammed shut again. The smoke and dirt whipped out through the cracks.

In the center of the floor, Xander crouched on his hands and knees, his shoulders rising and falling. His breathing was deep and fast.

"Xander!" David yelled. He dropped onto his knees in front of his brother, then reached out with his good arm and grabbed Xander's bicep. "Xander, downstairs—"

"Listen," Xander interrupted. He raised his face. It was scratched and filthy. His eyes were wide with excitement, rimmed with tears.

"We need you," David said. "Dad's—"

"Dae!" Loud. In his face. Xander rose up to grip David's shoulders. "I found her!"

David's lungs locked up. A tingling sensation coursed up his arms and over the back of his neck like electricity.

Xander leaned close. He said, "I found Mom!"

NOT THE END . . .

READING GROUP GUIDE

1. Xander wants to immediately plunge through the portals in search of Mom. Dad insists that they pace themselves; he says their search may take time, and he wants to make sure they have the energy and freedom to continue looking for as long it takes. Do you understand Xander's feelings? Do you see that Dad may be right as well? What can Xander learn from Dad's caution? What can Dad learn from Xander's impatience?

2. When David jumped through the portal, thinking he saw his mother, was he being reckless or heroic? What would you have done?

3. After David returns from the World War II French village, the old man Jesse wakes up realizing someone is in the house. What do you think happened that alerted him to the Kings' presence in their new home?

4. Why do you think Taksidian wants the Kings out of the house?

5. What's with that clearing? What do you think makes it defy the laws of gravity? Dad calls it a place to take your mind off everything. Do you sometimes need a mental break? What do you do to clear your mind?

6. Dad invited Xander into a calm, peaceful world, where they sat on a picnic blanket by a river. Why does Dad think that

this world may have contributed to his father's decision to give up their search and leave the house? What do you think this world is all about? Why is it relaxing when the other worlds seem to be so crazy?

7. Can you relate to David's experience at school that first day? Have you ever been the new kid in school? What did you do to adjust? Did anyone help? Why do you think bullies bully? What is the best way to handle bullies?

8. In the Mission Control Center, Xander puts up posters of tough-guy action movies to get them "psyched up" for their adventures into unknown worlds. What psyches you up to tackle difficult challenges?

9. David and Xander disobey Dad to go into the Civil War world. Xander says it's because Dad's search for Mom isn't moving fast enough. Do you agree that this is a good reason to sneak into the portals? With Mom's rescue at stake, what else could Xander have done?

10. Cops arresting Dad. Clayton coming into the house through the linen closet portal. Xander finding Mom (but he didn't bring her back!) What happens next?

11. Where would you like to see the Kings go? Your idea could end up in a future Dreamhouse Kings book. See the contest information page for more details.

THE HOUSE TALKS.
IT BREATHES. AND IT'S HUNGRY.

DREAMHOUSE KINGS
BOOK 3

gatekeepers

BEST-SELLING AUTHOR
ROBERT LIPARULO

"If you like creepy and mysterious, this is the house for you!"
— R.L. STINE, Author of the Fear Street and Goosebumps series

BOOK THREE OF
DREAMHOUSE KINGS

WHICH DOOR WOULD YOU GO THROUGH TO SAVE THE WORLD?

BOOK FOUR OF
DREAMHOUSE KINGS

ENTER THE LAST TWO
STORIES OF THE HOUSE.

ABOUT THE AUTHOR

ABOUT THE AUTHOR

Robert Liparulo has received rave reviews for both his adult novels (*Comes a Horseman, Germ, Deadfall,* and *Deadlock*) and the best-selling Dreamhouse Kings series for young adults. He lives in Colorado with his wife and their four children.